Love at last?

"Elizabeth!" Sam sprinted toward her with his heart in his throat. *Let her be OK,* he prayed. He was only a hundred yards away and closing in fast, but she looked as if she were about to topple over the edge.

"Elizabeth!" Sam grabbed her tightly from behind, and she collapsed back against his chest.

"I feel so dizzy," she murmured, turning in his arms to face him. Her beautiful blue-green eyes were dazed.

"Shhh, it's OK now," Sam said soothingly as he stroked her hair. "I've got you."

"Sam." Elizabeth rested her head against his chest and closed her eyes. "If you hadn't caught me . . ."

"But I did catch you, Elizabeth," Sam whispered. She lifted her head and looked up at him, her eyes shining with gratitude. He lowered his mouth to close the distance between them.

Bantam Books in the Sweet Valley University series.
Ask your bookseller for the books you have missed.

#1	COLLEGE GIRLS	#25	BUSTED!
#2	LOVE, LIES, AND JESSICA WAKEFIELD	#26	THE TRIAL OF JESSICA WAKEFIELD
#3	WHAT YOUR PARENTS DON'T KNOW . . .	#27	ELIZABETH AND TODD FOREVER
		#28	ELIZABETH'S HEARTBREAK
#4	ANYTHING FOR LOVE	#29	ONE LAST KISS
#5	A MARRIED WOMAN	#30	BEAUTY AND THE BEACH
#6	THE LOVE OF HER LIFE	#31	THE TRUTH ABOUT RYAN
#7	GOOD-BYE TO LOVE	#32	THE BOYS OF SUMMER
#8	HOME FOR CHRISTMAS	#33	OUT OF THE PICTURE
#9	SORORITY SCANDAL	#34	SPY GIRL
#10	NO MEANS NO	#35	UNDERCOVER ANGELS
#11	TAKE BACK THE NIGHT	#36	HAVE YOU HEARD ABOUT ELIZABETH?
#12	COLLEGE CRUISE		
#13	SS HEARTBREAK	#37	BREAKING AWAY
#14	SHIPBOARD WEDDING	#38	GOOD-BYE, ELIZABETH
#15	BEHIND CLOSED DOORS	#39	ELIZABETH ♥ NEW YORK
#16	THE OTHER WOMAN	#40	PRIVATE JESSICA
#17	DEADLY ATTRACTION	#41	ESCAPE TO NEW YORK
#18	BILLIE'S SECRET	#42	SNEAKING IN
#19	BROKEN PROMISES, SHATTERED DREAMS	#43	THE PRICE OF LOVE
		#44	LOVE ME ALWAYS
#20	HERE COMES THE BRIDE	#45	DON'T LET GO
#21	FOR THE LOVE OF RYAN	#46	I'LL NEVER LOVE AGAIN
#22	ELIZABETH'S SUMMER LOVE	#47	YOU'RE NOT MY SISTER
#23	SWEET KISS OF SUMMER	#48	NO RULES
#24	HIS SECRET PAST	#49	STRANDED
		#50	SUMMER OF LOVE

And don't miss these Sweet Valley
University Thriller Editions:

#1	WANTED FOR MURDER	#9	KILLER AT SEA
#2	HE'S WATCHING YOU	#10	CHANNEL X
#3	KISS OF THE VAMPIRE	#11	LOVE AND MURDER
#4	THE HOUSE OF DEATH	#12	DON'T ANSWER THE PHONE
#5	RUNNING FOR HER LIFE	#13	CYBERSTALKER: THE RETURN OF WILLIAM WHITE, PART I
#6	THE ROOMMATE		
#7	WHAT WINSTON SAW	#14	DEADLY TERROR: THE RETURN OF WILLIAM WHITE, PART II
#8	DEAD BEFORE DAWN		

Visit the Official Sweet Valley Web Site on the Internet at:

http://www.sweetvalley.com

SWEET VALLEY UNIVERSITY®

Summer of Love

Written by
Laurie John

Created by
FRANCINE PASCAL

BANTAM BOOKS
NEW YORK · TORONTO · LONDON · SYDNEY · AUCKLAND

RL 8, age 14 and up

SUMMER OF LOVE
A Bantam Book / August 1999

Sweet Valley High® and Sweet Valley University®
are registered trademarks of Francine Pascal.
Conceived by Francine Pascal.

Produced by 17th Street Productions,
a division of Daniel Weiss Associates, Inc.
33 West 17th Street
New York, NY 10011.

ISBN: 0-553-49270-5

Published simultaneously in the United States and Canada

PRINTED IN THE UNITED STATES OF AMERICA

OPM   0 9 8 7 6 5 4 3 2 1

To Nicole Pascal Johansson

Chapter One

"Who's up for the rattlesnake?" Todd asked, looking over the top of his menu at his teammates.

"Ugh! You've got to be kidding!" Pam exclaimed with an exaggerated shudder. "Rattlesnake meat? That's disgusting!"

For once I agree with Frizzhead, Jessica thought. She suppressed a shudder of her own and reached for her mug of coffee. It was Sunday morning, two days after the competition event at the Grand Ole Opry, and she and the rest of Team One were crowded into a booth at one of Nashville's funkier diners. "I'd rather eat cheap shoe leather," she said after a sip of the strong, hot brew.

"Why?" Todd asked reasonably as he put down the oversized menu. He picked up the salt-and-pepper shakers—miniature ceramic versions

1

of Kenny Rogers and Dolly Parton—and examined them closely. "Rattlesnake is considered a delicacy in Tennessee. Besides, I've heard it tastes like chicken."

"That's what they say about frogs' legs too," Tom chimed in. He grabbed the Dolly Parton saltshaker away from Todd. "And believe me, frogs' legs do not taste like chicken."

"You better watch where you're holding that saltshaker," Rob said with a loud guffaw.

Oh, brother, get ready for some stupid frat-boy humor! Jessica removed the well-endowed saltshaker from Tom's grasp and set it back down. Rob considered himself to be the life of the party. The fact that he was about as funny as a bad-hair day was obvious to everyone but him.

"So what *does* rattlesnake meat taste like?" Neil asked, pleating one of the red-and-white-checked napkins between his long, sensitive fingers.

"Probably considerably worse than it sounds," Jessica muttered, but nobody appeared to hear her.

"It couldn't possibly taste as sweet as my snookums," Rob murmured. He draped an arm around Pam and snuggled closer to her, forcing Neil, who was sharing their side of the booth, even deeper into a corner. Rob ducked his head to nibble on Pam's ear and ran a hand through her orange, permed hair.

2

"How can you even think of comparing me to a snake?" Pam squealed indignantly. She made a show of pushing Rob away, but it was clear she relished his attention.

If you ask me, the snake's the one that should be insulted! Jessica thought as she glanced across at Pam from underneath her long lashes. *I'm sure the average snake has way more personality, and it's got to have better legs!*

"Would someone pass the cream, please?" Jessica asked. She gestured toward the small, blue, spatter-ware jug at the other end of the table, but nobody paid her any attention. With a sigh she shifted uncomfortably in her seat and reached across Tom and Todd, nearly spilling the cream on their laps as she did. Sharing a small bench with a former football star and a basketball star was far from comfortable.

But that's the least of my problems, she thought. So far, her dream summer was not turning out as planned. In fact, as far as Jessica was concerned, the summer was more like a nightmare. She'd been so sure the Intense Cable Sports Network Competition was going to be a total blast, a chance to make some serious cash and meet some great people. All she had to do was drive across the country, compete in different events, and rack up points, which got converted into a cash prize at the end of the trip. But reality had a funny way of not living up to expectations. Not only was her team in last place, but as for meeting great people . . . Jessica rolled her eyes heavenward.

First she'd gotten stuck in the middle of the battle between Elizabeth's exes. She glared at Tom and Todd, who had started thumb wrestling. In the past weeks the two of them seemed to have morphed into Beavis and Butthead.

As if Watts and Wilkins weren't bad enough, she had to spend every day and night with the nightmare couple from hell. Her gaze flickered back to the nauseating sight of Pam and Rob wrapped in each other's arms. Rob had all the personality of a wet paper towel, and Pam had a voice that sounded like nails being dragged across a blackboard. Rob was slightly overweight, with stringy hair that always looked unwashed, and Pam's frizzy perm looked an awful lot like a clown wig. They had a disgusting habit of slobbering all over each other in public—when they weren't on the outs. The fact that Rob and Pam had found each other was proof that miracles did happen.

But as boring as Tom and Todd might be, as awful as Pam and Rob were, they were nothing compared to Neil Martin. Jessica slid her eyes across to the table. Neil was from Stanford. He was smart, funny, and totally gorgeous. He was so gorgeous, in fact, that Jessica had made a major play for him. There was just one problem. He was gay.

Jessica slammed her menu down on the scarred wooden table in irritation, her cheeks flaming in embarrassment as an image of her trying to put the moves on Neil flashed before her eyes. She'd been so sure Neil had been sending her romantic signals that she was totally unprepared for his bombshell. As if being rejected for the first time in her entire life wasn't bad enough, the shock of Neil's news had sent her reeling out into the night, only to be separated from her teammates and stranded in the wilds of South Dakota.

Not every male was immune to her charms, however. Jessica smiled as she remembered Elvis, the slick, gentlemanly guy with a gorgeous convertible Caddy who'd picked her up and dusted her off. After showing her a good time in Memphis, he'd helped Jessica return to her team. And at the Opry, after a dazzling duet with Jessica, Elvis had convinced her not to bail on the whole trip—and urged her to make up with Neil.

Jessica knew that she'd changed over the summer—before the road trip she would never even have considered apologizing to anyone—but her first experience saying "I'm sorry" had left a pretty bad taste in her mouth. Although Jessica had practically groveled in front of Neil and the other team members, their only response had been to fling her apology right back in her face.

Jessica's eyes shot fiery sparks at her teammate, but Neil appeared to be engrossed in studying the gold records that decorated the walls of the diner. And while Neil was totally ignoring her, her other teammates were treating her like a necessary evil—like somebody's annoying little sister or something. In spite of Nashville's sweltering heat the atmosphere around the breakfast table was positively glacial.

Everyone's treating me like I'm a total outcast. Jessica sighed disconsolately. *They're acting like I have the plague or something. Worse! They're acting like I'm wearing polyester!*

"Well, I'm going to try the rattlesnake," Todd announced as a waitress dressed like a country-and-western star approached the table. "After all, you only live once."

"I'll have it too." Tom nodded agreement. "In fact, I'll take a double order." He handed his menu to the waitress.

Jessica bit the inside of her cheek to keep herself from bursting out laughing. She couldn't get over the way Tom and Todd had been behaving since the team had left San Francisco, veering back and forth between being best buddies and mortal enemies. You didn't have to be Einstein to figure out that Tom was still trying to win Elizabeth back and that both he and Todd were trying to keep her out of the clutches of Sam Burgess, one of Elizabeth's teammates. Privately, Jessica didn't think they had a chance. From what she'd seen of Sam, he was way more manly and grown up than Tom Watts or Todd Wilkins would ever be.

"I'll skip the rattlesnake, but get me a cheese omelet and a side of pancakes," Rob said. He patted his rounded stomach. "I'm hungry today."

"For you, miss?" The waitress turned to Jessica.

"Uh, I'll just have some scrambled eggs and a side of bacon," Jessica said, momentarily dazzled by the flash of rhinestones embedded in the waitress's three-inch-long nails. She hadn't seen such big hair or such overdone makeup since the last time she'd stayed up late watching televangelists. Out of the corner of her eye she saw that Neil was having a hard time keeping a straight face too.

Just my luck. Jessica shook her head in chagrin. *The one person on the trip I could totally bond with, and we're not even speaking to each other!* Anger and resentment welled up in her, and she handed her menu back to the waitress with a sullen expression on her face.

"Anyone see the sugar?" Neil asked after the waitress had taken their orders and departed. He sipped his coffee and studiously avoided looking at Jessica. "There's got to be some little white packets with Wynonna Judd's picture on them around here." He twisted around in the booth to check the table behind them.

Jessica did not like being ignored. Tom and Todd were thumb wrestling again. Rob and Pam were kissing. Just perfect! In a burst of anger she grabbed the Dolly Parton saltshaker and dumped half of it in Neil's cup.

"I guess I'll have to wait until the waitress comes back," Neil said as he turned around and picked up his cup.

Jessica gave him a brilliant smile as he took a large sip. Neil gagged as if he were drinking poison and dropped the cup with an exclamation of surprise. The ceramic shattered in a million pieces, and hot coffee streamed all over the table and down the front of his pants. Pam squealed and jumped out of Rob's lap.

Jessica shook her head as she watched Neil dab frantically at his lap with the checked napkin. "Accidents will happen," she said sympathetically. *Yeah, they sure will,* she thought. *Especially when you ignore Jessica Wakefield!*

"I don't know," Elizabeth said slowly as she adjusted her sunglasses against the glare. She looked at Ruby with a small frown. "I think that one of the Division Street cafés might be a little too much for Charlie right now." *Poor Charlie,*

Elizabeth thought. She shook her head. *What a tough situation.*

"She's pregnant, not dying," Ruby replied, her voice tinged with irritation. She finished brushing her wild mane of dark, corkscrew curls and sat down next to Elizabeth on one of the stone benches that lined the perimeter of the RV parking lot. A small cropping of trees provided welcome relief from the intense sun, and a few flowers poked their way out from between the cracks in the cement. "A lot of celebrities hang down there. Charlie might really enjoy it. Besides, a good breakfast is probably just what she needs." Ruby reached into the pocket of her jeans for her favorite silver barrette and snapped it around her ponytail.

"That's true." Elizabeth bit her bottom lip as she considered what Ruby was saying. She unscrewed a tube of sunblock and, pushing up the sleeves of her turquoise polo shirt, began applying it to her lightly tanned arms. "But she is still sleeping. I think we should let her rest. It makes more sense to go get some takeout and bring it back."

"I guess you're right," Ruby agreed reluctantly. "Isn't there some saying about sleeping for two?"

Elizabeth smiled. "I think that's eating for two. But what do I know? I'm hardly an expert on pregnancy," she said softly as she smoothed some sunblock on her shapely legs, set off by the crisp white shorts she wore.

"It's hard to believe, isn't it?" Ruby shook her head in amazement. "It's like one of those things you read about that happens to strangers but never to anyone you know. I mean, it's not the end of the world or anything, but . . ."

"At least Scott's a total sweetie," Elizabeth said. "Unlike Sam," she muttered.

Elizabeth and Sam had been running hot and cold all summer. But Friday night they'd gone from sizzling to arctic in a matter of moments. They'd been in the middle of a major kissing session when both of Elizabeth's ex-boyfriends had interrupted them. Sam's reaction had not been all that it could have been. He'd simply walked away from the whole scene, leaving her to face the deadly duo of Tom Watts and Todd Wilkins all by herself. The next time she'd seen him was when he and Josh had burst in on her, Charlie, and Ruby, crying over Charlie's situation. At the sight of the three women in tears, Sam had reacted in a typically sexist way and Elizabeth had told him to get lost—for good. Now, in the clear light of day, Elizabeth was amazed that she had ever been attracted to anyone so cruel.

It's like he's some kind of Dr. Jekyll and Mr. Hyde. She shook her head wonderingly. *One minute he's a fantastic guy, not to mention a fantastic kisser, and the next . . . wham! No more Mr.*

Nice Guy. All of a sudden he's the poster child for the pig-of-the-month club!

"Hey, Ruby, Elizabeth." The object of her thoughts sauntered over with Josh and Uli in tow. "What's going on?"

Elizabeth avoided Sam's eyes and concentrated on a small pebble near her foot, but Ruby turned to face him.

"We were deciding where we should go get breakfast," she said. "I want to go down to Division Street, but Elizabeth thinks we should just get some quick takeout. Charlie's still asleep. She's . . ." Ruby paused and glanced at Elizabeth, who nodded imperceptibly. "She's not feeling well," she finished.

"Well, I think Liz is right," Sam said. He plucked a blade of grass from the base of one of the trees and began to chew on it. "We should let Charlie sleep."

Elizabeth looked up in surprise. She hadn't expected Sam to be so sensitive to Charlie's needs. Usually he ragged on Charlie pretty badly. She gave him a small, very tentative smile. She couldn't help noticing as she did so how handsome his face looked in the early morning light.

"Yeah," Sam continued, crossing his arms over his chest. His wrinkled T-shirt and baggy cargo pants couldn't disguise his trim yet muscular build. "I don't think we should wake her up."

11

"That's really thoughtful of you . . . ," Elizabeth began.

"'Cause if we do," Sam continued, "she'll take forever to get dressed, you three will spend ages yakking over what she should wear, and we won't get over to Division Street, much less be done with breakfast, for at least an hour and a half."

"Yeah," Josh said, tucking a stray strand of carefully oiled hair back into place. "We want to get on the road soon. We're in first place. Let's make sure we keep it that way," he added, an angry frown twisting his features. "Not that I care about the five-thousand-dollar prize money or anything. But I don't want to fall behind again and end up in last place with only some stupid gift certificate to some totally bogus old-person store to show for my summer." He looked between Sam and Elizabeth. "C'mon, we could have gotten out of here yesterday. And besides, who knows what Savannah holds?" he finished.

Savannah was the next destination on the contest route.

"Maybe it would just be the easiest, *ja?*" Uli asked in his lilting Swedish accent. He looked hopefully at Elizabeth.

"I have no problem with getting takeout," Elizabeth muttered. *I just have a problem with vain, insensitive men.*

"Great, so everybody is OK together." Uli nodded, his blue eyes sparkling in obvious relief. Elizabeth flashed him a small smile. She'd come to appreciate Uli's easygoing personality over the past few weeks. He seemed to have a calming, civilizing effect on Sam, unlike Josh, who appeared to bring out the very worst in Mr. Burgess.

"There's a diner half a block from here. Elizabeth, why don't you and Ruby walk on over there and pick up some eats for us all," Sam said, grinning lazily. "Josh and I will take a look at the map, see if we can figure out the best places for pit stops."

"Fine," Elizabeth said shortly. She didn't feel up to arguing with Sam—again. "C'mon, Ruby." She sprang to her feet and pushed passed the guys. Ruby followed.

"Hey," Sam called after her. "Don't forget to get me some jelly doughnuts."

I guess Mr. Hyde's back in town, Elizabeth thought grimly. She tucked her purse under her arm and, pointedly ignoring Sam, walked off in the direction of the diner.

"Hey, watch where you're going!" Todd cried out as the Winnebago swerved sharply. "You almost missed that turnoff." He looked up from the map he was holding and regarded Tom with concern.

"Sorry," Tom mumbled. His hands gripped the steering wheel so hard that his knuckles turned white. "My mind was on other things." *Yeah, like how beautiful Elizabeth looked when she was lip-locked to Sam!* His heart sank inside him at the memory, and his deep brown eyes flashed with pain.

"Well, keep it on the road," Todd replied shortly. "The last thing we need is an accident."

"You guys need help?" Neil poked his face between the two front seats. "I'm just doing some crossword puzzles." He gestured toward the back of the Winnebago, where Jessica was reading a magazine and Pam and Rob appeared to be napping. "If you want to take a rest, Tom, I'd be happy to get behind the wheel."

"I'm fine," Tom said between clenched teeth. "Guys, in case you didn't notice, I didn't miss the turnoff. You don't have to treat me like I'm some kid with a learner's permit who's taken his dad's Mercedes out for a joyride. So back off."

Neil quirked a questioning eyebrow at Todd, who shook his head and went back to studying the map spread out across his lap.

"OK." Neil shrugged. "Whatever you say." He turned around and made his way unsteadily back to his bunk.

"You'd think I just ran twelve red lights or something," Tom muttered under his breath. He reached for the can of soda that was resting on

14

the dashboard and took a long swig. "I'm perfectly capable of handling this thing in my sleep. There's nothing wrong with my driving."

But there's a whole lot wrong with my love life. Tom resisted the urge to bang his head against the steering wheel. Instead he settled for draining his soda and crumpling the metal can in his fist. *If only it were Sam's head,* he thought, grimacing.

"How could a beautiful, brilliant girl like Elizabeth Wakefield fall for a guy like Sam?" he asked, shifting his attention from the road to Todd. "He's irresponsible, sloppy, lazy—and those are his good qualities!"

"Will you watch it!" Todd cried out. He grabbed the wheel and wrenched it to the right, narrowly avoiding a collision with an eighteen-wheeler.

"You haven't answered me." Tom claimed the wheel again and deftly navigated the Winnebago into the right lane. "Why do you think Elizabeth is so hung up on Burgess? He's got nothing—"

"Hey, we're not going to go through this again, are we?" Todd sighed. "Because if we are, you can let me off at the next gas station. I'd rather hitchhike to Savannah."

"Chill, OK?" Tom lowered his sunglasses and glared over the rims at Todd. "I'm not the only one here who has a problem with Burgess. You weren't that thrilled to see your ex-girlfriend in the clinch either."

15

"That's different," Todd replied stiffly. "I don't want to see Elizabeth get hurt, but I'm not still hung up on her the way you are. Anybody ever tell you to get a life, buddy? You're totally obsessed with Elizabeth. And she made it pretty clear in Nashville that she's not still obsessed with you. Maybe it's time you moved on."

"Yeah," Jessica called from the back of the Winnebago, where she was curled up on one of the twin beds. "Face it, Tom. As far as Elizabeth's concerned, you're about as current as last year's hemlines. I'm sure you'll never find anyone as fabulous as my sister again," Jessica drawled as she flicked through the glossy pages of her magazine, "but you could probably dredge up somebody halfway decent."

Tom looked up at the rearview mirror and flashed Jessica a look of extreme irritation. In his opinion, taking relationship advice from Jessica Wakefield was like taking advice from a politician on how to be honest.

"Look, all I'm saying is that there are other women out there," Todd went on as he reached for his own can of soda.

"Like Dana?" Tom asked snidely, still burning with embarrassment from Jessica's unsolicited comments.

"You better watch where you're headed, Watts." Todd's voice was angry. "And this time I don't just mean the road."

"Sorry." Tom pushed his sunglasses back on his nose. "Forget I said anything, OK?" He sighed as he tossed the crumpled soda can over his shoulder in the direction of the overflowing wastebasket that stood near Jessica's twin bed.

"Hey, be careful!" Jessica complained, jerking to a sitting position as the can whizzed by her nose.

"What are you talking about?" Tom said as he glanced at Jessica in the rearview mirror. The sight of her blond hair flying about her shoulders as she hastily moved out of missile range made his heart contract with longing for Elizabeth. "That missed you by a mile. It was a perfect shot! I'd like to see you beat that," he joked feebly to Todd. But Todd ignored him and maintained a stony silence as he looked out the window at the passing scenery.

Tom rolled his eyes and cursed inwardly. He was not up for an argument with Todd. The bond they'd forged over the past few weeks was tentative at best, and right now, especially after last night's setback, Tom was feeling like he needed Todd on his side.

Most times Tom couldn't get over the fact that he actually wanted Wilkins in his camp. When he first found out that he would be on the same team as Elizabeth's ex-boyfriend, it had almost been enough to make him bail. Only the thought of spending every day with Elizabeth

17

had made him stick around. Of course, that wish had gone up in smoke when Tom realized the wrong Wakefield twin would be sharing his Winnebago. Still, Tom thought as he stole a look at Todd—who was still pointedly ignoring him— Wilkins turned out not to be such a bad guy. At least, most of the time.

There was still plenty of tension between them. The fact that Todd was Elizabeth's ex-boyfriend was pretty hard to bear, and things weren't made any easier by Todd's being heavily involved with Dana.

Dana Upshaw was Tom's ex-girlfriend. Although in his heart of hearts Tom had never been that serious about Dana, she hadn't seen things that way, and their breakup had been pretty messy. Tom wasn't sure what exactly Todd knew about his relationship with Dana, but he did know that whenever her name came up between them, it was as if someone had thrown a bucket of cold water on the conversation.

Why did I have to mention Dana? Tom asked himself. *And more important, why can't I just accept what Todd's telling me and let go of Elizabeth? What's* wrong *with me?*

"Listen," Tom began as he slowed down to make a right turn onto a back road. "You're right, there are other women out there. And after finding Liz with Sam the other night, I came pretty close to giving up. But it's no use. I woke up this morning wanting her just as badly as ever. I just can't seem to get over Elizabeth! I want her back, Todd. I have to prove to her that I'm more of a man than that Burgess creep."

Jessica cackled loudly, and Tom shot her a fierce look to shut her up. She turned away, chastised.

"Hey, I understand." Todd turned from the window and gave Tom a rueful smile. "I was under Elizabeth's spell for a long time too. There was a time when I wanted to have your head on a plate. I felt about you the way you do about Sam. But things change."

"Yeah." Tom nodded slowly. He signaled that he was turning left. "Things change, all right. I never thought that I would see my ex-girlfriend kissing another guy that way. Man, it was intense!" Tom punched the steering wheel with his fist. "She never kissed me like that!"

"Yeah, it was definitely hot," Todd agreed, sighing. "I think the last time Elizabeth kissed me like that was the night before we left for college. And that's only because she was so carried away by the fact that our lives were about to change forever."

"Elizabeth kissed you like she was kissing Sam?" Tom turned to stare at Todd in horror, as if Todd had just admitted that he and Elizabeth used to rob banks together. Todd was laughing so hard at the expression on Tom's face, he didn't even notice that Tom wasn't looking where he was driving.

"How often did she kiss you like that?" Tom asked frantically. "You said that was the *last* time. How many times were there before that?" He looked at Todd, aghast, the road completely forgotten.

"What's going on?" Neil demanded, rushing up to the front of the cabin and pushing Todd roughly out of the navigator's seat. "What are you bozos doing?" He grabbed the wheel from Tom and steered them away from the tree they were about to plow into. "Where are we anyway? This doesn't look like the interstate!"

Tom was silent as he took control of the wheel again and stared out the window at the marshy swampland that surrounded them. He had to admit that Neil was right. It didn't look like the interstate.

"What's happening?" Rob asked grumpily. He wiped the sleep from his eyes as he wandered toward the front of the Winnebago. "What's going on out here? You didn't get us lost, did you, Watts?"

"I . . . ," Tom began helplessly.

"From what I overheard of the conversation," Neil said dryly, "I'd say that Watts is completely, totally lost."

With a groan Tom brought the Winnebago to

a stop on the side of the road, and put his head in his hands.

Ruby frowned slightly as she sat cross-legged on her bunk and flipped through the pages of one of her top-forty songbooks. None of the tunes caught her eye. She was more in the mood for an old-fashioned ballad than any of the current hits—or any of the heavy songs she'd been working on this summer. With a sigh she tossed the book back into her guitar case.

"Any objection to Bob Dylan?" She quirked an eyebrow at Elizabeth and Charlie, who were sitting at the dining table, sipping glasses of canned lemonade.

"Sounds fine to me," Charlie said pleasantly, slipping on a pair of glasses she rarely wore. Ruby figured all the crying Charlie had done lately had ruined her eyes for contacts this morning. "I remember my parents playing his records all the time."

"Uli?" Ruby looked over at him. His wiry frame was draped over his bunk, where he was writing a letter to his family back in Sweden.

"It's not a problem." Uli flipped his blond hair out of his eyes and smiled at Ruby.

Ruby nodded and began strumming her guitar. The tension she'd felt inside since Charlie had delivered her bombshell began to ebb away as her fingers plucked the chords.

The soulful lyrics and bittersweet melody were incredibly soothing, and Ruby smiled as she sang. She could tell that the music was having a similar effect on her teammates. Charlie hummed along, and Elizabeth tapped her feet in time with Ruby's strumming.

"Hey, could you keep it down back there?" Josh called from the driver's seat. "I can't concentrate with all that caterwauling going on."

Ruby's cheeks flamed in humiliation. She stopped singing abruptly and gave Josh a dirty look in the rearview mirror.

"I think Ruby's playing is lovely," Charlie interjected into the strained silence. She put down her lemonade and smiled at Ruby. "It's also highly entertaining."

"Well, it's giving me a headache," Josh rudely insisted.

"It didn't seem to be giving you a headache when Ruby helped put us in first place," Elizabeth shot back.

Ruby flashed Elizabeth a grateful smile. When Ruby had first met her, she'd been sure that Elizabeth was nothing more than a southern California airhead, a living, breathing Barbie doll. The kind who had her future all mapped out, even down to what silver pattern she would choose when she got married. But Elizabeth had surprised her more than once. Maybe she wasn't the most adventurous, fun-loving girl around, but she was one of the most fair-minded.

"Yeah, OK, Ruby helped us win with that Naomi and Wynonna Judd duet you guys did," Sam called from the front, where he was navigating. "But remember what happened in Twin Falls?" He turned around in his seat and stared accusingly at Ruby. "If you hadn't jumped out of the boat, we wouldn't have been disqualified from that event."

"That's totally out of line, Sam." Elizabeth flung the words out before Ruby had a chance to respond. "That was a really dangerous situation, and it's totally inappropriate of you to be dwelling on the fact that we lost some points. Ruby might have died! Get a little perspective. And let it go, OK? It's over."

"Thanks, Elizabeth. But let's get the facts straight, once and for all. I did not *jump* out of the boat!" Ruby's voice shook with anger as she put down her guitar and sprang to her feet. "It was an accident!" She marched purposefully toward the front of the Winnebago, undeterred by Charlie, who reached out to stop her.

"Hey, calm down." Sam put his hands up in a placating gesture.

"Why should I?" Ruby demanded. Her brown eyes shot fiery sparks at Sam, and her hair fairly crackled with electricity. "Ouch!" she cried as Josh swerved left, causing her to lose her balance and slam into the back of Sam's seat.

Sam reached out to steady her, but she

pushed him off. "Elizabeth's right," she said with her hands on her hips. "You were way out of line."

Sam shrugged. "Look, I'm just pointing out the truth. Maybe you didn't mean to take a dive in Twin Falls, but the reality is you did, and we lost the event. So it's even more important that we keep our heads up in Savannah. That's all I'm saying."

"Well, all I'm saying . . . ," Ruby began.

"C'mon, you guys, let's not argue," Elizabeth said reasonably. "We're all on edge. I think we could use a pit stop."

"I know I could," Charlie called from the dining table. "Do we have one scheduled soon, Sam? Maybe Josh could use a break from driving too."

"I am getting kind of tired," Josh admitted grudgingly as he pulled over to the side of the road. "Maybe you can take over until we stop for lunch," he said to Sam.

"Sure." Sam slid out of the navigator's seat and into the driver's seat. "If you can hang for another forty minutes, we can make it to Chattanooga."

"This sounds very good to me," Uli called from his bunk. "I'm most hungry."

"Me too," Charlie seconded.

"What about you, Ruby? Are you into taking a break?" Elizabeth asked.

24

Ruby paused, unsure of what she should say. It was clear that everyone was waiting for her to go along with the plan, and she was grateful to Elizabeth and Charlie for defusing the tension, but she was still pretty chapped over Josh's nasty comments about her playing and Sam's reminding her—yet again—of how she'd screwed up in that earlier event. Unfortunately she knew from past experience that she was unlikely to get any kind of satisfactory apology from either of them.

She shrugged in silent agreement and made her way toward the back of the Winnebago, where Charlie poured her a glass of lemonade.

I didn't mean to bail in Grand Rapids, but maybe I should now! Ruby thought as she sat down at the dining table and took a swallow of the lukewarm lemonade. *It's not as if anybody around here appreciates me. Maybe I should just pack up my guitar and hit the road. After all, Elizabeth's right. I did do pretty well at the Opry. I know the music is more important than the fame, but . . . I am supposed to be all about taking life as it comes, taking chances. . . .*

Ruby eyed her guitar longingly as fantasies of being discovered filled her head again. So Josh didn't appreciate her music—so what? Ruby was sure there was an audience out there just waiting for her. Maybe it was time for her to find it.

*　　　*　　　*

"Where are we?" Rob asked querulously. He looked from Tom to Todd, but Todd just looked at him blankly, and Tom's face was buried in his hands.

"We're somewhere in between dazed and confused, but hey, we just might have made it all the way to hopelessly lost," Neil said as he brushed his shaggy black hair out of his eyes with a sigh. He looked out the window, trying to get some idea of where they'd ended up, but the murky swampland that Tom had driven them into didn't offer any clues.

"Sorry, guys," Tom said quietly. His face was beet red, and if Neil hadn't been so irritated, he might actually have felt sorry for him.

"Yeah, well, what's done is done." Neil shook his head. "I know you guys were mighty wrapped up in discussing Elizabeth Wakefield's extracurricular activities, but the next time I offer to drive, you might want to take me up on it."

"I will, I will." Tom groaned. "Do you want to drive now?" he asked hopefully.

"Do you think it might be a good idea?" Neil said sarcastically. Tom vacated the seat, and Neil slid behind the wheel. "I'll need some help navigating, especially since we don't have a clue as to where we are." He turned the key in the ignition and nodded at Todd. "You probably want to join Tom in the back. Rob? You up for it?" He glanced at Rob over his shoulder.

26

Rob shook his head. "Sorry, Neil, but I just woke up. I think I'm too wiped to be useful. I'll probably just make things worse." He looked over his shoulder at the back of the Winnebago, where Pam was snoring blissfully. "And I think Pam's out of the running too."

"That leaves you, Jessica," Neil said flatly. He didn't relish the thought of being stuck up in front with Jessica Wakefield for the next few hours. Things were still too raw between them. It was clear from her scowl that Jessica was in no mood to make up either. Last night's blowup had been pretty horrible. Neil had walked away, vowing not to make one more conciliatory move in her direction. She was vain and egotistical and . . . and Neil was shocked to realize he still missed her.

Neil just couldn't figure Jessica out. After all, she wasn't the one who'd swallowed half a cup of salt with her breakfast. His luminous gray eyes watered at the memory, but he couldn't help smiling at the memory of her feisty revenge.

"What are you laughing at?" Jessica snapped. She climbed into the navigator's seat and smoothed her short, sleeveless, pink-and-white polka-dotted dress over her thighs.

"Nothing," Neil replied shortly. Part of him did want to make up with Jessica, but part of him was afraid. What if there was something more behind Jessica's antics than seriously wounded vanity? What if . . . what if something else were bothering her? Something deeper.

Is Jessica homophobic? Neil asked himself with a small shiver. He hated to think that anyone he liked as much as Jessica—in her happier moods—could be that small-minded, but still, she'd started acting seriously strange right after he'd told her that he was gay. And Neil had to admit his accidentally dissing her on national TV during the Cubs versus Dodgers game—and their confrontations since—hadn't exactly helped smooth things over between them.

"Now what?" Jessica asked. A frown marred her beautiful face. "How am I supposed to read this map when I don't even know where we are?"

"Just give me a second to get out of this marshy area," Neil responded as he turned the Winnebago around. "If we can get back on anything resembling a road, we should be able to pick up the interstate."

"Easier said than done," Jessica said petulantly. She reached up and began to play with the pair of fuzzy dice that Rob had tied to the rearview mirror after the team had placed last in Las Vegas.

"Hey, what are you doing?" Neil complained. "You're supposed to be helping me, not blocking the view!"

Jessica sighed loudly and slumped down in her seat, the map dangling uselessly from her fingers.

"Do you think that you could at least open the map?" Neil asked testily as he turned left onto a dirt road.

Jessica pretended to spread the map open on her lap, deliberately wrinkling it as she did so. "It's too crinkled. I can't read it," she announced. She crumpled the map in a ball and tossed it on the dashboard.

"Could you at least try, Jessica?" Neil's voice was tight with irritation. "We're already halfway back to civilization," he said as the dirt road turned into a respectable four-lane highway. "If you'd help out just a little, we should be able to get back on track pretty soon."

Jessica shrugged and ignored the map. She opened the window and stuck her head partway out.

Neil sighed dramatically. "Fine, be that way."

He had reached across the dashboard to grasp the map when a sudden gust of wind blew through the cabin. Jessica's long, blond hair whipped across his face. He put his hand up to untangle himself from the silky strands—and the map flew out the window!

"Catch it!" Neil cried as the map took off.

"Too late now," Jessica said smugly.

"Great." Neil hit the wheel in frustration. "Before, we were only hopelessly lost. Now we're completely, irretrievably lost."

"What's the problem?" Jessica shrugged,

unfazed. She flipped open the glove compartment and rifled through it until she found a package of chewing gum.

"What's the problem?" Neil looked at her as if she had sprouted horns. "The problem is, how are we going to get where we're going? Ever think of that? No, of course not. Ms. Wakefield only thinks of herself. Never the good of the team."

"Where *are* we going?" Jessica said, ignoring his cut and unwrapping a stick of gum.

"Savannah. No." Neil frowned. "Atlanta. We're spending the night in Atlanta and driving to Savannah early in the morning."

"Why didn't you say so before?" Jessica asked around a mouthful of chewing gum. "It's totally easy to get to Atlanta."

"Oh, really?" Neil regarded Jessica suspiciously. *She must just be yanking my chain,* he thought. *No way does she know how to get us out of this one.*

"Really." Jessica nodded. "See that designer outlet store about a hundred yards down the road?" She pointed a slender arm out the window.

"Yeah?" Neil said dubiously. "What about it?"

"Turn left at that store and go about a mile and a half until you reach the Gaudicci outlet. From there it's about three miles to the Ralph Lauren outlet. You can follow the trail of the designer discount stores all the way to Atlanta." She flashed him an arch look. "I heard all about the road to Atlanta from my sorority sisters."

Neil shook his head in admiration as he turned left at the outlet. Jessica could be a real pain, but she was also quite a character. He missed their friendship. *Maybe I should just swallow my pride and make up with her,* he thought. *Maybe.*

Chapter Two

"There should be someplace to stop right around here," Sam announced as he turned off the highway and onto one of the smaller roads that led into Chattanooga. He glanced in the rearview mirror to see what everyone thought of his announcement, and his heart stopped for a second at the sight of Elizabeth busily scribbling in some kind of journal. Her beautiful face was partially obscured by her long, blond hair, but her delicate profile was visible, and it was impossible not to notice the way the turquoise polo shirt she wore molded itself to her slim curves.

Get over it, buddy, Sam berated himself. With an effort he forced his eyes back on the road and began looking for a good spot to have lunch. *Remember how much of a pain she can be.* But while he knew that was true, he couldn't stop thinking of their kiss the other night.

Sam frowned in irritation as he tried to push all thoughts of Elizabeth out of his mind. He shifted gears, and as he did so, he felt the photograph of his ex-girlfriend that he'd stuck in the pocket of his chinos that morning crumple slightly.

Sam knew he should be happy that Angelina was waiting for him down in Florida. But for some reason, the thought of Angelina in her string bikini failed to distract him. When he'd started out on the road trip, he'd been eagerly anticipating hooking up with her. He figured that they had a perfect arrangement. There was a lot of mutual attraction and, since Angelina lived all the way across the country, very little chance of his getting tied down. Problem was, he just wasn't looking forward to seeing her as much as he had been. He was . . .

Whoa, hold up, guy, Sam told himself sternly. *You're letting this Wakefield thing get way out of hand. You didn't even like Elizabeth at first, and besides, she's not exactly being too friendly now!*

Sam knew that he was partly at fault for Elizabeth's current behavior—he hadn't behaved all that well when her dweeby ex-boyfriends had found them kissing Friday night—but Elizabeth's attitude hadn't been all that it could have been either. She'd practically groveled in front of them, as if they'd caught her doing something wrong. *As if she was ashamed to be seen with me.*

Sam frowned. You just couldn't trust women. And what had she ever seen in those guys anyway? They both seemed like the worst kind of airhead jocks. Sam had to admit that they were kind of good-looking—in a really stupid kind of prep-school way.

But as bad as that scene had been, things had gotten distinctly worse. A few hours later he and Josh had come in on Elizabeth, Ruby, and Charlie in the midst of some kind of girl bonding session. Sam had made an especially stupid, cutting remark. He winced a little at the memory of it.

Sam wondered why he even cared. He was always up for a little romance, but anything major just wasn't his style. He hadn't come on the trip to get heavily involved with anyone. See the country, score some major bucks, have a little fun. Why not? But commitment? No way. Especially not commitment with a serious, studious, responsible type like Elizabeth. A girl who dated Mr.-Big-Men-on-Campus types. Types against which Sam knew he could never hope to compete.

"Here looks like a good place," Uli said, interrupting Sam's train of thought. He walked up to the front of the Winnebago and pointed out the window to a small roadside hamburger stand.

Sam looked out the window at the pretty picnic

tables covered by blue-and-white bandanna-style cloths. "Seems OK. At least there's shade." He gestured at a cluster of willow trees with graceful, drooping branches that shielded the tables from the blistering sun.

"OK? It's better than that," Josh declared as Sam pulled the Winnebago over on the shoulder of the road. "I can't wait to see how far I can spit!"

"Excuse me?" Charlie and Elizabeth called in unison from the back of the RV.

"What are you guys talking about?" Ruby asked as she straightened her legs and stretched the kinks out of her back.

"Tobacco-spitting contest," Uli said as they all piled out of the RV. He pointed at a sign by the side of the road.

Elizabeth pushed her sunglasses up on top of her hair and regarded the sign dubiously. "Bob's Bodacious Burgers," she read.

"Best burgers in the south," Charlie continued, bemused. "Spit tobacco farther than fifteen feet and win a free cheeseburger and unlimited root beers."

"But the burgers are only a dollar fifty, and it costs a dollar to buy the tobacco!" Ruby exclaimed as she stepped closer to read the fine print.

"Who cares? I'm up for it," Josh announced loudly. He reached into the pockets of his

miraculously wrinkle-free khaki pants and sauntered over to the stand to buy some tobacco.

"Are you into it?" Sam raised an eyebrow at
Uli.

"I am learning to chew tobacco from my
grandfather in Sweden, back when I am little."
Uli grinned. "I'm going to win much root beer."
He followed Josh over to the stand.

Sam shrugged noncommittally. He didn't
really care one way or another, but he was in the
mood for a burger, and something as ridiculous
as tobacco spitting might just be the thing to
take his mind off Elizabeth. "I guess I'll try it,"
he said as he scratched his unshaven jaw.

"I think I'll just pay for my root beer, thank
you," Charlie said with a laugh. "What about
you guys?" she asked, turning to Elizabeth and
Ruby.

"Spitting isn't quite my style," Elizabeth said
as she walked toward the stand. She stumbled
slightly on a small pebble and went crashing into
Sam. He reached out a hand to steady her, but
she pushed him away forcefully.

Sam couldn't help grinning at the look on her
face. Maybe spitting wasn't Elizabeth's favorite
thing to do, but right then she looked like she'd
be plenty happy to take aim at him. His hands
tingled where they'd briefly connected with hers,
and he shoved them into his pockets.

"Why don't you grab us a table, Charlie?"

Ruby said. "Elizabeth and I will get the food. We can sit in the shade and watch these guys make fools of themselves." She smiled at Uli, who was busy chewing a giant wad of tobacco. He and Josh were standing by the side of the road directly across from the picnic tables.

Sam paid for some tobacco and went over to join them. He stuck a piece in his mouth and nearly gagged at the noxious taste.

"What's up with Elizabeth?" Josh asked around a mouthful of tobacco. "You two seem on the outs again. Is she still upset about the other night?"

Sam paused. Josh didn't know about the little dustup with Wilkins and Watts. He was referring to when he and Sam had walked in on the girls crying. "I guess I was a little insensitive," Sam admitted.

"Are you kidding?" Josh asked incredulously. "What did Elizabeth expect you to do? Whip out a hankie and join them? Maybe she thinks you should take up embroidery too!" He chewed his tobacco vigorously. "Why are you so into her anyway? You've got that girl waiting in Florida. Most guys would give their right arm for an opportunity like that. It's a sure thing."

Maybe he's right, Sam told himself, but he got an empty feeling in the pit of his stomach when his eyes drifted over to the picnic tables, where Elizabeth was laughing with Ruby and Charlie.

She looked incredibly pretty with the soft breeze stirring her golden hair.

Maybe he's right, Sam repeated to himself. *And anyway, maybe Elizabeth will come around. We've had plenty of bad moments on this trip already. And we've gotten over them.*

"I'm ready," Uli yelled. He positioned himself near a thin red line that had been painted on the asphalt and let fly with a major wad of tobacco. It sailed cleanly past the second red line painted fifteen feet away. Uli bowed as the girls clapped and cheered.

"My turn." Josh's olive complexion flushed in triumph as his wad of tobacco also flew past the marker. "He shoots, he scores!" Josh whooped as he jogged off to claim his free cheeseburger.

"Guess that just leaves me," Sam muttered as he moved toward the marker. He closed his eyes for a second and chomped down on the tobacco. Then he spit the tobacco as hard as he could.

"Oh!"

At the sound of Elizabeth's cry, Sam's eyes flew open. Then they widened in shock as he realized what he had done. When he'd closed his eyes, he'd missed seeing Elizabeth get up from the picnic table—and walk right into his line of fire!

Uli and Josh were laughing hysterically. But Elizabeth's eyes shot daggers at Sam as she wiped the tobacco juice off her cheek.

Sam didn't know what to do. He was torn between laughing along with the guys and rushing to her side. But one thing he did know for sure. It didn't seem likely that Elizabeth would be "coming around" anytime soon.

Charlie adjusted her red gingham, peasant-style blouse as she walked behind the hamburger stand in search of a pay phone. The blouse, which had been somewhat loose when she'd bought it at the beginning of the summer, was now uncomfortably tight. *And something tells me it's not because it stayed in the dryer too long,* Charlie joked feebly. She knew the real reason her blouse was too tight. Who would've figured that she'd already be getting bigger? Charlie anxiously glanced down at her stomach. Thankfully, she wasn't really showing yet. The casual observer wouldn't notice anything, but to someone who knew her body as well as she did herself . . .

Charlie heaved a deep sigh. Scott knew her body as well as she did. That's why she was sure her news wouldn't come as a total surprise. They'd discussed the possibility after she'd been so sick in Chicago, but still, there was a world of difference between calmly discussing a possibility and confronting your boyfriend with a certainty.

How do I tell him that I'm pregnant? Charlie gnawed fretfully at her lower lip. Although she loved and trusted Scott, she was dreading the upcoming conversation. She pressed a hand against her stomach to calm the butterflies that were flitting about in mad circles. She was feeling nauseous, and this time the cause wasn't morning sickness. Charlie was more nervous at this moment than she'd ever been in her entire life.

"C'mon," she told herself as she swung open the glass door to the phone booth. "Scott loves you—he can handle this. You can handle this." She reached into the pocket of her denim shorts for some change and quickly dialed Scott's cellphone number.

"Charlie?" Scott answered on the first ring, and Charlie felt a wave of relief wash over her at the eagerness in his voice.

"It's me." She nodded even though Scott couldn't see her. She twisted the phone cord as she stared mindlessly at the rest of the team seated at the picnic tables.

"What's happening? Do you feel any better?"

Charlie took a deep breath. "Well, yes and no. Scott, remember I told you that I was worried?"

"Yes," Scott said, his voice low. Charlie closed her eyes and conjured up an image of him. She wanted to be in his arms so much right then. "Is it what you thought?" he went on.

"Yes, it is. I'm pregnant, Scott." Charlie could

hear his sharply indrawn breath and wondered nervously what was going through his mind.

"I guess you kind of suspected, huh?" Scott asked softly.

"Uh-huh," Charlie whispered. "Oh, Scott, what are we going to do?" Vaguely she was aware of Ruby strumming her guitar. A melodic love ballad floated through the air.

"Sounds like Ruby," Scott commented.

"You can hear that?" Charlie asked in surprise. And then she felt annoyed. Was *that* what Scott was thinking about? Ruby's singing? She frowned.

"Yeah. It's a love song, right? Good," Scott said gently. "Charlie, I don't know what we should do, but I do know that I love you."

Charlie's brow cleared at Scott's reassuring words. Of course, they still had a pretty big problem to deal with, but at least she could count on her boyfriend's love. "Oh, Scott," she whispered caressingly. "I love you too."

"Do we have some time to think about this?" Scott cleared his throat. "I mean, if we decide to do anything radical . . ." His voice trailed off.

"We have time," Charlie said simply. She knew what Scott meant—if they decided to have an abortion—and she wasn't at all sure how she felt about it.

"Well, then, let's just take things slowly," he said. "Call me tomorrow, OK?"

"OK." Charlie smiled into the phone. "I love you, Scott."

"I love you too, Charlie," he said.

She hung up the phone and walked back toward the picnic tables with a spring in her step.

"You look pretty happy," Elizabeth commented. She shifted on the bench to make room for Charlie.

"I guess I'm feeling a little better." Charlie nodded and took a sip of her root beer.

"Did you tell him?" Elizabeth asked quietly, a look of sympathy in her blue-green eyes.

Charlie was touched by Elizabeth's obvious concern. She knew that Sam and Josh thought Elizabeth tended to act like a mother hen, but Charlie appreciated her thoughtfulness.

"Was he OK about it? What did he say? Does he think that you should bail?" Ruby asked, putting down her guitar. "I mean, some of the events in this contest can be pretty dangerous. The white-water rafting was totally scary. Who knows what might happen in Savannah?"

Charlie frowned for a second. What had Scott said, exactly, besides telling her that he loved her? They hadn't even discussed the contest. *Should* she cut loose? She knew that Ruby was itching to head out on her own with her guitar, but Charlie wasn't sure that she herself wanted to leave the team. Sure, the white-water rafting had been terrifying, but she could also remember how exhilarating it had been to face down her fears. She shifted in her seat, aware that Ruby and Elizabeth were waiting for an answer. Suddenly she was uncomfortable under their close scrutiny.

"Did the tobacco juice stain your blouse?" she asked Elizabeth, anxious to change the subject.

Elizabeth scowled as she fiddled with the wrapper from her straw. "Yes, but thanks for asking," she muttered darkly.

"Maybe you should cool it with Sam," Charlie said suddenly, surprised by the sour expression on Elizabeth's normally sunny face. "Look, I know that bad boys like Sam can seem really sexy, but they're usually more trouble than they're worth."

"What do you mean, cool it?" Elizabeth said, biting into a french fry. "There's nothing to cool. There's nothing going on between me and Sam."

Charlie exchanged a small wink with Ruby. It seemed impossible that Elizabeth would still be denying there was something going on between her and Sam. But she was, for whatever reason. Well, Charlie thought, maybe Elizabeth was deceiving herself, but she wasn't deceiving anyone else on the team. Sometimes the sexual tension between Sam and Elizabeth was so thick, you could cut it with a knife.

"Whatever you say." Charlie swiped one of Elizabeth's fries. As she sat there under the beautiful willow tree, eating lunch with two new friends, listening to their conversation, Charlie suddenly felt completely exhausted. *Who am I to give Elizabeth relationship advice!* she thought, shivering slightly in the mild breeze. *I'm pregnant, and I'm not even married!*

"Atlanta!" Pam squealed in excitement as she tumbled out of the Winnebago into the RV parking lot. "It's just like I pictured it. So *Gone With the Wind*!" Her freckled face was flushed with excitement.

"I don't really see what a boring parking lot has in common with *Gone With the Wind*," Jessica said dryly as she easily smoothed the wrinkles out of her cotton-Lycra-blend dress. But she was relieved that the rest of the team was no longer treating her like a leper since she'd gotten them back on the road to Atlanta. And she had to admit that what she could see of the city beyond the parking lot looked unusually pretty. The sun was shining brightly, and the air was heavy with the scent of peach blossoms.

"Oh, don't you get anything?" Pam pouted and trailed her wrist up and down Rob's biceps. "This is where they have all those houses they used in the movie. We could visit Tara, snookums. We could stand where Rhett told Scarlett that he loved her and—"

"I think that 'Tara' is on the Paramount lot in Los Angeles," Tom cut in hastily, much to everyone's relief. Pam had no compunction about spilling extremely personal details about her relationship with Rob to anyone within earshot.

"The woman who wrote the book lived here in Atlanta, though," Neil offered helpfully as he rolled up the sleeves of his blue oxford shirt and loosened the collar. "Margaret Mitchell. Maybe you want to take a look at her house. I'm sure there are guided tours."

"Perfect!" Pam clutched at Rob's sleeve. "Let's get going."

"What time do we have to be back?" Rob asked quickly. Jessica hid a smile. It was obvious he wasn't into going on a guided tour. Pam's eyes flashed in irritation.

"Whenever," Jessica responded. She hoped Pam and Rob wouldn't get into one of their fights. Watching them make up afterward was a truly nauseating experience. "We're staying in Atlanta tonight and driving to Savannah in the morning. It's not too long a drive."

"Then there'll be time to hit the bars tonight!" Rob punched the air with his fist. "Awesome! Let the party begin!" He hurried out of the parking lot, dragging Pam behind him.

Tom nodded at Todd, who was busy stretching the kinks out of his back. "You want to go and check out the CNN headquarters?"

"I'd rather watch paint dry," Todd replied.

"But maybe we could go visit a plantation or something."

"Well, I'm going shopping," Jessica announced as Tom and Todd began to walk away. She reached into her purse for a tube of lip gloss and a small hand mirror and went to work on her face.

Jessica hadn't bothered with much makeup for most of the trip—just the basics, like pressed powder, mascara, and lipstick. It was definitely a new experience for her. But it was one thing to be stuck in an ugly Winnebago without a fully made-up face and quite another to go out in public and shop with a naked face. She examined her reflection critically and was pleased to see that although it had been weeks since she'd had a facial or a trim, her skin looked flawless and her hair was as lustrous as ever.

Not that there's anyone around to appreciate my finer points, she thought disconsolately as she glanced at Neil. They were the only two left in the parking lot, and Jessica had the feeling that Neil was waiting around to see what she would do.

He doesn't expect me to apologize, does he? Jessica snapped her compact shut with a sniff. *Well, he can wait forever. Been there, done that, bought the T-shirt!* Still, Jessica couldn't help feeling a bittersweet tug at her heart as she looked at Neil. They had had a great time hanging out together on the first part of the trip, and she was sure it would be more fun wandering around Atlanta with him than all by herself.

Neil took an uncertain step toward her, and Jessica held her breath. *Maybe he's going to apologize to me!* she thought with a small tremor of excitement. But Neil abruptly turned left and headed out of the parking lot.

"Fine, see if I care," Jessica called after his departing back. She tossed her hair and followed him out of the RV lot.

"Which way should I go?" Jessica muttered. Her brow furrowed as she considered the various options. She knew from Lila that Buckhead was the most exclusive district in Atlanta, with shops and stately homes to rival those of Beverly Hills. But Little Five Points was the hippest area, with plenty of hot clubs. It was a little early for the club scene, though, so Jessica cheerfully headed toward the shopping district.

Jessica felt her heart lifting as she walked down the beautiful, tree-lined streets. Although she'd enjoyed some of the wilder contest events, especially the white-water rafting, and the all-too-brief time she'd spent with Elvis, her personal savior, she'd missed her usual quota of shopping. South Dakota hadn't exactly been a shopper's paradise, and Memphis and Nashville were too country-western. But Atlanta . . . Jessica felt almost dizzy with excitement as she stared at the row of expensive boutiques that were set out in front of her like a line of exquisite bonbons.

She paused outside a curio shop, looked in the window, and caught her breath at the beautiful display. Delicate china figurines nestled among silver-topped perfume bottles, Victorian-style jewelry, and other unusual bibelots. The whole window simply screamed class. And it was totally unlike any store Jessica had ever seen back in Sweet Valley.

"This would be the perfect place to find a one-of-a-kind souvenir," she whispered as she pressed her face against the glass. "I wonder how that mother-of-pearl inlaid picture frame would look on my dresser? I know just the photo of me to put in it!" Jessica murmured. No sooner had she spoken than a hand reached in from the back of the window and removed the picture frame from the display.

"No!" Jessica cried in dismay. "It's mine!" She dashed into the shop—and came face-to-face with Neil.

"You can't have that!" she exclaimed.

Neil was holding the frame up to a light. He turned to face Jessica and quirked an eyebrow. "Why not? It's for sale, isn't it?" he asked the clerk hovering nearby.

"That's not what I meant, and you know it," Jessica spluttered as Neil calmly reached for his wallet.

"Hey, I was here first," Neil said coolly. "Now, if you had been willing to apologize to us—and to me—we could have gone shopping together and you might have seen the frame first." The clerk rang up the sale and handed Neil the frame wrapped in tissue paper. Neil smiled at Jessica and sauntered out of the shop.

"That does it!" Jessica fumed. She could take Neil not being interested in her as a woman. She could handle the fact that he was gay. She could even get over the fact that he and the other team members still hadn't apologized for leaving her behind in Wonderlust, South Dakota. But she would *not* forgive him for outshopping her!

"Hey, what's that?" Josh cried as Elizabeth swung left out of Chattanooga and toward the interstate.

"Lookout Mountain?" Charlie scrambled off her bunk and joined Josh at the side window. "I've heard of that place," she said.

Elizabeth looked briefly at the sign Josh had pointed out. "Best views in the south," she murmured. "Follow the arrows up the seventy-three-degree incline. Seventy-three degrees! That ought to be some view," Elizabeth admitted. "But sorry, guys. It's out of the way."

"Oh, come on," Josh said, coming into the front cabin, where Ruby was navigating next to Elizabeth. "It's got to be awesome."

"Yes, I think we should check it out," Uli seconded.

"Forget it," Sam said abruptly. "We don't have time if we want to get to Atlanta by dinner."

Who's Sam to decide what we can and can't do? Elizabeth thought with a flash of irritation. She glanced at him in the rearview mirror. *And why does he have to look so cute when he's such a mess?* she wondered, even more irritated by her attraction to him than by his overbearing attitude. She rubbed the side of her face where the tobacco had landed. *If any other guy had done that to me, I would have killed him,* she thought grimly. *But I let Sam get away with it. I didn't even ask him to replace my new blouse!* The realization brought a scowl to Elizabeth's face.

"Lookout Mountain sounds really cool," Ruby said, glancing up from the map. "And who says that we have to be in Atlanta for dinner? I'm with Josh and Uli. I think that we should go."

Ruby's siding with Josh? Elizabeth was amused. That *had* to be a first.

"Besides, we don't have to stop in Atlanta," Josh added. "We can drive straight through to Savannah, get there about midnight, and sleep in the RV lot there."

"It's not a good idea," Sam insisted stubbornly. "Have you guys forgotten that we're in the middle of a contest? If we drive straight

51

through to Savannah, we may be too tired to-morrow morning to really focus on the training session for the event."

"Sorry, Sam, but that's a really lame excuse," Charlie said with a giggle.

"It sure is," Elizabeth muttered under her breath. She quickly turned left toward the signpost for Lookout Mountain.

"Yes!" Josh high-fived Ruby, then looked slightly embarrassed by his emotional outburst.

"Why are you turning?" Sam demanded. He glared at Elizabeth.

Elizabeth didn't reply. *Actually, I have two very good reasons for turning,* she thought as the Winnebago began the steep ascent. She was pleased to see Josh and Ruby getting along, and she thought it might be a good idea to encourage them. The fact that Sam was so clearly against going up the mountain was like icing on the cake.

After all, Elizabeth thought with a satisfied smile, *how many times do you get to do a good deed and make yourself happy at the same time?* She suppressed a mischievous giggle as she glanced at Sam in the rearview mirror. Maybe being forced to take a sightseeing detour didn't rank up there with having tobacco spit all over you, but from the furious expression on Sam's face, it wasn't a bad substitute at all.

*   *   *

"Want to rethink the CNN option? I have a feeling paint drying might be a whole lot more interesting than this," Tom said as a gaggle of sorority girls pushed their way past them and into the plantation's souvenir shop.

"Yeah, it is kind of a tourist trap," Todd agreed. He paused at the door of the shop and plucked a frilly parasol from its stand. "But is it really me?" he asked anxiously, twirling it over his head.

"You're a nut." Tom laughed, grabbed the parasol from Todd, and put it back in the stand. "Let's get out of here, OK? I feel like a drink. How about a couple of mint juleps?"

"I don't know." Todd fell into step beside him as they walked out onto the broad verandah of the mansion. "They're pretty strong."

"Afraid we can't handle our liquor?" Tom smirked. "C'mon, mint juleps are a southern tradition. Besides, William Faulkner used to drink them all the time."

"Uh, your point would be . . . ?" Todd smiled. "And yeah, I know we can handle drinking, but we do have an event scheduled tomorrow. Personally, I hate to compete with a hangover."

"Gotta agree with you on that one," Tom said. "I wonder what the event will be anyway." He hoped it would be something he could really shine in, something that would allow the team to pull ahead, something that would allow him to really impress Elizabeth. "It better be something that gets us out of last place."

"You're not kidding," Todd said ruefully. "I came on this trip to have some fun and pick up some bucks, not just to drive across the country in a Winnebago with the most nauseating couple alive. And I hope it's something challenging too, not like guzzling ice water in Wall Drug. Look, I'm not up for mint juleps, but I am thirsty. How about getting something less strong to drink?" He gestured toward a small café that was set up near a gazebo on the mansion's front lawn.

"Why not?" Tom walked along, focused on Todd's previous comment. *What if the event is too challenging?* he wondered. *What if I screw up? How am I ever going to win Elizabeth back, especially after Friday night's disaster!* He heaved a deep sigh as they sat down at one of the wrought-iron tables.

"What?" Todd looked at him quizzically. "This place too girlie for you?"

"I guess it is, kind of," Tom said, taking in the flowered napkins and lacy place mats. "But that's not what's bothering me."

"Let me guess." Todd flipped open the menu. "You're either really bummed because they're out of watercress sandwiches, or you're still worrying about how you're going to get Elizabeth back before the trip is over."

"Is it that obvious?" Tom said in surprise. "I mean, that I'm always thinking about her?"

Todd burst out laughing. "Buddy, it couldn't be more obvious if you were wearing a sign around your neck." He smiled at the look of chagrin on Tom's face.

Tom paused for a second, unsure of how much he should confide in Todd. The two of them had forged an uneasy bond over the common goal of keeping Elizabeth out of Sam Burgess's slimy clutches, but that didn't necessarily mean that Tom always felt comfortable with Todd. He was hanging with him now more out of habit than anything else. Still, he had to admit that they were having a pretty OK time. And Todd hadn't ragged on him too badly after he'd gotten them all lost. Maybe spilling some of his fears to Todd wouldn't be such a bad idea.

"What should I do?" he asked Todd.

"You really want to know what I think?" Todd signaled the waitress. "I think that you should pay attention to what Elizabeth said the other night. I think you should get over her."

"I can't do that!" Tom protested.

"You mean, you won't do that," Todd corrected. "Look around you. There are a lot of smart, pretty girls in the world." He dropped his voice and inclined his head toward one of the adjacent tables. "See that girl over there?"

Tom followed Todd's eyes to where a lovely

southern belle was daintily sipping an iced tea. Her long, dark hair was swept up into a French twist, and her pale pink linen suit was impeccable. Delicate high-heeled sandals emphasized her long, shapely legs.

"What about her?" he asked as the waitress came over. "Well?" he demanded after they'd ordered and the waitress had departed.

"I think she likes you." Todd smiled.

"Are you crazy?"

"No, really, she's looking at you. She probably thinks you're cute," Todd insisted.

"Really?" Tom asked.

Todd shrugged. "Hey, some girls have weird taste."

Tom adjusted the collar of his button-down shirt and tried to look sophisticated. He flashed what he hoped was a suave smile at the beautiful, chic girl.

The girl flashed a dazzling smile in return. Tom's heart leaped to his throat as she got up and began to walk seductively in his direction.

"What did I tell you?" Todd whispered, elbowing him in the ribs.

Tom was lost in a dream as the girl came toward him. He could already picture how beautiful she would look in her traditional, lacy wedding dress. They would get married here in Atlanta, and then they'd move back to California and she would . . .

"Oh, Martin!" The girl flung herself into the arms of a guy who was so buff, he looked as if he had been chiseled from marble. His bulging biceps threatened to split the thin, expensive material of his shirt as he wrapped his arms around the girl.

Tom turned back to Todd with a blistering look.

"OK, so I was wrong. Sue me," Todd said, fighting back laughter. "Listen, forget her. What about Jessica? She seems available. I thought she was after Neil, but that doesn't seem to be happening."

"You've had too much sun, Wilkins." Tom took a swig of the iced tea the waitress placed in front of him.

"No, really," Todd insisted. "You obviously have a thing for the Wakefield women. Besides, Jessica can be a real prima donna, but she's not all bad all the time, is she?"

Tom shrugged. "I guess you're right. I mean, since she's been on this trip, she only changes her outfits once a day instead of the usual five times. And OK, so she doesn't spend hours each morning doing her makeup. Maybe only an hour. And yeah, she didn't totally bail when she got ditched in South Dakota. She did finally figure out a way to meet up with us—and she did do a fabulous duet with that Elvis guy, even if it didn't count for the team. But . . . but . . ." Tom trailed off. *But she isn't Elizabeth!*

*   *   *

"What's cotton candy?" Uli asked. He sniffed suspiciously at the fluffy pink mass Charlie had just handed him.

"It's artificial color, sugar, and a couple of chemicals thrown in. It actually tastes pretty good." Sam laughed at the dubious expression on Uli's face. He was enjoying Lookout Mountain more than he'd expected. The view was spectacular, and it didn't hurt that they'd stumbled onto some kind of county fair. He'd placed first in the sack race, and Uli had won a stuffed animal at the ring toss.

"It's most delicious!" Uli said as he scarfed down a mountain of the pink foam.

"Glad you like it," Sam said. "But don't go thinking it's the best cuisine America has to offer, OK?" Sam smiled and wandered over to where Ruby and Josh were trying their luck at the ring toss.

"How's it going?" he asked Josh, who was frowning in concentration.

"I keep missing," Josh complained. "Must be the altitude."

"Sure." Sam laughed. "I bet that's exactly what it is." He drew in his breath sharply as he looked at the surrounding mountaintops. "It is incredible up here," he said as Josh's toss went wide of the mark.

"It really is," Ruby agreed. "Hey, congratulations on the sack race. What did you win?"

"Three feet of black licorice rope." Sam grinned, patting his pocket. "Want some?"

Ruby shook her head. "No, thanks. I'm holding out for the bubblegum ice cream."

"Nailed it!" Josh whooped. "Where do I collect my prize?"

"Over by the caramel apples," Uli said as he and Charlie joined them, his hands covered in pink sticky stuff.

"Hey, that's a really cute puppy." Josh waved at the stuffed toy under Uli's arm. "I hope they have more. I could give it to my next girlfriend. Girls love puppies." He grinned and dashed off toward the caramel apples.

Too bad we don't get along like this all the time, Sam thought wryly. *We'd probably ace the competition if we did!*

"Hey, has anyone seen Elizabeth?" Ruby asked. "I want to ask her if she'll do the wheelbarrow race with me."

"She was with me a few minutes ago," Charlie said. "But she wandered off. I think she wanted to check out the view."

Sam turned away from the group and scanned the horizon. He had a sudden urge to be with Elizabeth. Everyone was having such a blast and putting away their differences at last. He couldn't help feeling that it would be a shame if he and Elizabeth couldn't do the same. After all, he probably should apologize to her for having walked off and left her with Tom and Todd. . . .

"There she is," he murmured. She was standing at the very edge of the mountain, silhouetted against the sky. She looked both beautiful and serene. He didn't think he'd ever before seen her in a moment of quiet reflection like this, and he swallowed hard at the vision she made.

"Hey, isn't she a little close to the edge?" Charlie said nervously.

She is awfully close, Sam realized with a frown. And then he noticed that she was looking extremely unsteady all of a sudden . . .

"Elizabeth!" Sam sprinted toward her with his heart in his throat. *Let her be OK,* he prayed. He was only a hundred yards away and closing in fast, but she looked as if she were about to topple over the edge.

"Elizabeth!" Sam grabbed her tightly from behind, and she collapsed back against his chest.

"I feel so dizzy," she murmured, turning in his arms to face him. Her beautiful blue-green eyes were dazed.

"Shhh, it's OK now, Elizabeth," Sam said soothingly as he stroked her hair. "I've got you."

"Sam." Elizabeth rested her head against his chest and closed her eyes. "If you hadn't caught me . . ."

"But I did catch you, Elizabeth," Sam whispered. She lifted her head and looked up at him, her eyes shining with gratitude. He lowered his mouth to close the distance between them.

"Are you guys OK?" Uli demanded breathlessly as he and the rest of the team rushed up.

"Do you need to sit down?" Charlie asked.

"Of course she does!" Ruby cried.

"Let's give her some air," Josh said.

"Yeah. You should sit down." Sam's face was masklike as he released Elizabeth abruptly.

That was pretty close. Too close. He laughed hollowly to himself as he shoved his hands in his pants. *I didn't really want to kiss her again anyway,* he told himself. But he couldn't help wondering why his arms felt so empty as he watched Ruby and Charlie lead Elizabeth away.

Chapter
Three

"Stand by your man . . . ," Elizabeth sang quietly in tune with the radio as she sped along the deserted back roads of the Georgia countryside. She gave a small smile as she glanced in the mirror toward the back of the Winnebago, where the rest of the team was cozily snuggled in their bunks. It was well after midnight, but after spending all afternoon at the fair, Sam and Josh had insisted that they push through to Savannah, and for once the rest of the team had been in agreement. The only problem was that while Sam and Josh were raring to get to Savannah, they were too tired to drive there. Uli was feeling ill after gorging himself on cotton candy and caramel apples, and Charlie and Ruby were totally spent from participating in every contest the fair had to offer.

"So guess who gets to drive," Elizabeth grumbled. But she didn't really mind. It was nice to have some time to herself for a change. She flicked off the radio and rolled down the window. The night air was completely still, and the soft, magnolia-scented breeze wafted through the cabin and ruffled her blond ponytail.

"Mmmm, it smells like heaven," she whispered as she struggled out of her SVU sweatshirt. The skimpy pink tank top she wore underneath left her arms bare. The warm air felt delicious as it caressed her skin. She purred with pleasure. "It feels like someone's trailing a gossamer silk scarf over my arms," she whispered.

No, that's not what it feels like. The thought slammed forcefully into Elizabeth's head. *It's different. It's like how Sam's arms felt when he caught me. Totally comforting . . . and at the same time . . . totally sexy.*

Now, what made her think a crazy thing like that? Elizabeth scowled as she glanced back at Sam's sleeping form. Sam Burgess was nothing but trouble. She'd been trying to figure him out for weeks, and she'd gotten nowhere. One minute Sam treated her as if she were a precious gift. The next, as if she were dirt. So what if his kisses were sweeter and more exciting than any she'd ever experienced? So what if the way he'd caught her when she swooned was like something straight out of a romance novel? He was also thoughtless, arrogant, and completely . . . "Oh!"

Elizabeth gasped in dismay as the engine sputtered

and the Winnebago ground to a halt. She knit her brows in confusion. It couldn't be another flat tire, and there was no way the engine was overheated. She glanced at the dashboard and groaned when she saw that they'd been running on empty. "Why didn't I check the tank when we left Chattanooga?" Elizabeth reprimanded herself. But the question was rhetorical. She knew why she hadn't bothered to check. She'd been too flustered by the conflicting feelings Sam had aroused in her to think responsibly. OK, he'd dashed to her rescue like a knight in shining armor. But that didn't make up for the way he'd treated her after their kiss in Nashville—just walking away—or the fact that he'd spent the rest of this afternoon ignoring her and hanging with Josh, probably laughing about the girl-friend he had tucked away in the Keys.

Oh, who cares about that now! Elizabeth thought. She tossed her head angrily. The important thing was that they were in the middle of nowhere with an empty gas tank. She drummed her fingers nervously against the steering wheel. "Wait a minute," she muttered, frowning in concentration. Hadn't she seen a gas station about a mile back? Elizabeth breathed a sigh of relief as she yanked the keys out of the ignition and moved as quietly as possible to the utility closet in the back of the Winnebago. She reached inside for the plastic gas can and walked back toward the door.

"Just what do you think you're doing?" a voice hissed as a hand closed over her wrist.

Elizabeth turned, startled. Sam's face was only inches away, and his eyes bored into hers with an intensity that made her shiver.

"I was just going to get some gas," Elizabeth said as she jerked her hand away. Her arm tingled where he had touched her. She was aware that she was blushing as if he'd caught her doing something wrong, and she ducked her head, hoping that it was too dark for him to see the rosy flush that tinged her cheeks.

"No, really?" Sam drawled. He crossed his arms in front of his bare chest. "You mean you're not on your way to a garden party?" He gestured toward the gas can. "I figured that was the latest style in hats. Maybe I should rephrase the question. What I meant to say was, are you crazy, sneaking out of here alone in the middle of the night?"

"I'm trying to make sure that we get to Savannah on time," Elizabeth said stiffly. She brushed past Sam and yanked open the door.

"Well, I'm not letting you walk along the deserted back roads of Georgia by yourself at one-thirty in the morning," Sam said over his shoulder as he walked over to his bunk and grabbed a shirt. "I'm coming with you," he announced.

Elizabeth nodded mutely, too tired to protest, as she watched Sam slip the shirt over his head. She wasn't in the mood for being alone with Sam, but she was relieved that she wasn't going to be trudging along the empty road by herself, with only the gas can for company.

"C'mon," Sam whispered. "Before the others wake up." He strode over to the door and hopped nimbly to the ground. "Let me take that." He reached for the gas can as Elizabeth joined him. "Did you see a gas station, or were you just hoping to get lucky?"

"I saw one about a mile back," Elizabeth said, falling into step beside him. "Why are you still whispering?"

Sam shrugged his broad shoulders. "I don't know," he murmured quietly. "I guess because the night air feels so soft, I didn't want to disturb it."

Elizabeth sucked in a breath. He'd surprised her again with his sudden sensitivity! She studied his face surreptitiously as he walked beside her. His T-shirt and jeans were rumpled, but there was no denying that he looked extremely sexy—almost beautiful—with the moonlight shimmering on his tousled sandy hair and bathing his face in its silvery beams.

Sam turned to look at Elizabeth, as if he was aware of her scrutiny. His hazel eyes twinkled with starlight, and his lips parted in a small smile. Elizabeth wondered if he was going to kiss her again. She wasn't sure that she wanted him to. As delicious as their last embrace had been . . .

"Are you familiar with Keats?" Sam asked abruptly.

"You mean John Keats? The English Romantic

poet?" Elizabeth replied in confusion. The image of Sam's kissing her rapidly dissolved. "Of course I am. Why?"

"Do you know his poem about St. Agnes Eve?" He quirked an eyebrow. "Young virgins might have visions of delight," he quoted softly.

Elizabeth swallowed hard, grateful that the darkness hid her expression. There was something extremely intimate about the way Sam recited the words—and the words too were powerful.

"And soft adorings from their loves receive," Sam continued, his voice dropping. "Upon the honeyed middle of the night." He paused and inhaled deeply. "I don't think I ever really understood that line before now, but this must be the kind of night that Keats was talking about. The air even smells like honey."

"I think it's magnolia," Elizabeth said, studying him from underneath her lashes as he walked along, swinging the gas can back and forth. *What a mass of contradictions he is!* She shook her head wonderingly. *One minute he's nasty and sarcastic. The next he's quoting exquisite poetry! How many guys my age have memorized Keats anyway?*

"It was almost worth getting out of bed in the middle of the night just so I could finally understand that line of the poem," Sam said, interrupting her train of thought.

"Thanks for coming with me," Elizabeth said sincerely.

Sam flashed her a crooked, self-conscious grin. "Hey, just because I stupidly insulted you girls the other night doesn't mean that I'm a total cad."

Could have fooled me, Elizabeth thought with a flash of annoyance. Still, Sam was being so considerate now, going with her to get the gasoline. Why wasn't he leaving her to fend for herself as usual? Was it because she really did mean something to him after all? Her heart fluttered against her ribs at the thought.

"This must be it." Sam veered right toward the small gas station by the side of the road. "Could you fill this up?" he said pleasantly to the attendant.

"Sure thing," the man said around a mouthful of chewing tobacco, hauling himself out of an old wicker rocking chair.

"You folks run out of gas?" He gave Sam a none-too-subtle wink. "Mighty pretty stretch of road to run empty on." He elbowed Sam in the ribs and guffawed.

"How much do I owe you?" Sam asked coldly.

Elizabeth hid her surprise. Sam was often more than willing to be a little vulgar. But maybe that was just because Josh brought out the worst in him.

Sam handed the money over to the clerk. "C'mon, Elizabeth, let's get going." He groaned slightly as he hoisted the can to his shoulder.

Elizabeth couldn't help noticing the impressive swell Sam's tanned biceps made under his T-shirt.

For a second she wished that he would put down the can and wrap his arms around her. *Are you crazy?* she chided herself. *You know he's bad news! Don't let a little moonlight and magnolia totally warp your judgment!*

"How are you holding up?" Sam asked.

"Fine," Elizabeth murmured.

"You seem a little tired," Sam said earnestly. "I probably won't be able to fall back asleep now. Do you want me to drive? We should reach Savannah in about an hour anyway."

"Sure." Elizabeth nodded. "I could use a break. Thank you." She gave him a small smile. She was itching to get back to the Winnebago, but she had no intention of crawling into her bunk and sleeping. She needed some time alone with her journal. *I've got to figure this guy out,* she vowed. *I have to sort out my feelings for him, and I won't be able to sleep until I do!* As Elizabeth gazed at Sam's strong profile, she had a sinking feeling that she wouldn't be sleeping anytime soon.

"Hey, guys, the instructions are here," Tom cried excitedly as he bent down and picked up the large manila envelope that had been pushed under the door of the Winnebago. The team had decided against sleeping in Atlanta. Instead they had driven through to Savannah and arrived late the night before. "The ICSN crew must have dropped them off when we were sleeping," he said as the rest of the team assembled around him.

"What do they say?" Todd asked after a giant yawn.

"Gimme a second." Tom eagerly tore open the envelope. His brow furrowed in concentration as he scanned the instructions. "It's a Civil War reenactment," he announced. "With paint guns and authentic reproduction costumes."

"Paint guns?" Jessica wrinkled her nose. "That sounds kind of icky."

"I think it sounds like fun," Tom replied. "Teams One and Four play the North and Teams Two and Three play the South." His heart skipped a beat as the meaning of the words sank in. *Maybe I could ambush Elizabeth and take her prisoner,* he thought, grinning at the idea. *She'd have to be impressed that I'm such a good soldier! Plus it would give us some time to talk privately.*

"Where does this all take place?" Neil asked, looking over his shoulder.

"I want to play a general," Rob insisted. "I've actually made a thorough study of the battle plans of a few Civil War generals."

"We don't have to follow a predetermined battle plan." Tom smirked at the crestfallen look on Rob's face. "Today's training session has been set up in a field about a hundred miles down the road," he said, turning to Neil. "And the event itself will take place in Skidaway Island State Park."

"What's the training session about if we don't have to follow a predetermined battle plan?" Todd asked.

"Target practice with the paint guns," Neil read out loud. "Because the objective tomorrow is to shoot as many people or take as many prisoners as possible."

"We just face off against the other side?" Rob asked with a frown. "No strategy?"

Todd took the instructions from Tom. "No. The Southern troops, Teams Two and Three, assemble at a designated point in the park, and the Northern troops, Teams One and Four, lie in ambush."

Perfect! Tom crowed to himself.

"When the starter gun is fired, Teams Two and Three try to smoke us out and Teams One and Four shoot from their hidden positions." Todd looked up from the pages he was reading.

"Can't we talk about the event later?" Pam whined. "I'm hungry. Where's breakfast?"

"The ICSN vans are here," Todd said, looking out the front window. "They've set up tables with coffee and doughnuts."

"Let me at 'em!" Rob yanked open the door and hopped out, closely followed by the rest of the team.

The parking lot was jam-packed. The ICSN crew was out in full force, and members from the different teams were milling about or converging on the buffet tables that had been set up. The smell of freshly brewed coffee and warm doughnuts, muffins, and scones filled the air, and there was a feeling of excitement as everyone talked loudly about the upcoming event.

Tom fished in his jeans pockets for his sunglasses and adjusted them against the blinding early morning rays. He looked around to see if he could spot Elizabeth. He was actually feeling pretty good about this event. He'd been on the archery team in junior high, and he figured he'd be able to handle a paint gun pretty well.

I'll rack up some points for the team and ambush Elizabeth, he thought with a satisfied smile. And then he'd have her alone, and they could really talk about their relationship. "How hard could this paint gun thing be?" he muttered as he went to score some doughnuts. *Paint guns are probably easier than a bow and arrow. It's probably like playing darts. You just take aim and wham!* Tom smiled as he recalled all the times that he'd played darts with his roommate, Danny Wyatt. "Hey, speak of the devil," he said as he spotted Danny drinking a cup of coffee near his team's Winnebago.

"Danny!" Tom called. But his roommate didn't hear him. He appeared to be particularly absorbed in talking with a cute girl from one of the other teams. Tom grabbed a couple of jelly doughnuts from the table and headed over to join his friend.

Wait until he hears how I intend to ambush Elizabeth, Tom thought. *Show her what a real man can do!* But his grin faded as he got closer to Danny. His roommate was totally wrapped up in his conversation with the girl. In fact, Tom couldn't remember the last time he'd seen Danny looking so happy. Just last semester Danny had been miserable about his own broken relationship with Isabella Ricci, and the two guys had bonded pretty strongly in their shared unhappiness.

How come he's having such a good time? Tom wondered. He stared at Danny from a distance. *Who is this new girl? Why isn't he still pining away over Isabella?*

Everyone seemed to be getting on with their lives, Tom thought ruefully. All of a sudden he had no desire to tell Danny about his plans to take Elizabeth prisoner. Instead he turned away in embarrassment.

"Sorry," Tom said as he bumped into a girl running in the other direction. "Elizabeth!" he cried.

"It's me, Tom." Jessica giggled at him. "Boy, you should have seen the look on your face when you thought I was Elizabeth. You've really got it bad," she said sympathetically as she grabbed one of his doughnuts. "Listen, Tom, even Elizabeth Wakefield isn't worth moping over this long! Hey, see you in the training session!"

Maybe I am getting a little mush brained, Tom

thought as he munched thoughtfully on his doughnut and watched Jessica dash away. *Everyone's treating me like I'm a puppy dog, not a man!* He finished the doughnut and threw away his napkin. He'd made up his mind. He'd had enough. He was going to ace this event, and not just so he could get Elizabeth alone. It was about time people realized Tom Watts was nobody's doormat!

"Civil War reenactment?" Ruby raised her eyebrows and stared at Elizabeth, who was holding the manila envelope of instructions. The team was clustered outside the Winnebago, eating breakfast and soaking up the sunshine.

"I don't know if I like the sound of that," Ruby continued. "I mean, war is totally bogus to begin with." She was feeling kind of crabby after Josh had accidentally stepped on one of her songbooks and gotten footprints all over it. True, it had fallen off her bed and onto the floor, but if he hadn't been in such a rush to score some free doughnuts, she wouldn't be stuck looking at Jewel's lyrics through a haze of muddy sneaker imprints. He hadn't even apologized.

Elizabeth nodded and took a sip of coffee. "I agree, but this might be fun. Teams Two and Three play the South, and Teams One and Four play the North." She flipped through the instruction pages. "And the points are added up at the end."

"What are paint guns?" Charlie frowned as she took the pages from Elizabeth.

"They're just like regular guns, only they shoot exploding paint pellets instead of bullets," Sam explained as he took a look at the printed instructions. "See, that's how the officials can tell who shot whom. Each team uses different-colored paint bullets. We're green."

"And Team One is red," Elizabeth said. "Team Three is yellow, and Team Four is blue. That's easy enough. You get more points if you shoot someone— kill them—than if you just take them prisoner."

"It seems more exciting than the singing event," Uli said. "It's really like living American history, *ja*? Besides, I was champion at skeet shooting back in Sweden."

"I get to be our general," Josh announced, slicking back his hair and sticking his sunglasses on top of his head.

"Who says so?" Ruby flashed him a challenging look. She didn't like the way he just assumed that he would get to be the leader.

"Do you want to be our general, Sam?" Josh asked.

"Not me." Sam shrugged and looked amused.

"What about you, Uli?" Uli just shook his head. "There, you see?" Josh said triumphantly. "Nobody else wants to do it."

"Who says the general has to be a guy?" Ruby challenged.

"That's right," Elizabeth said seriously. She sipped her coffee and looked at Josh. "Who says the general has to be a guy?" she repeated calmly. "Maybe Ruby wants to be the general."

"Maybe I do." Ruby crossed her arms over her chest and stared Josh down.

"Well, OK," Josh said suddenly. "If it means that much to you, sure."

"Huh?" Ruby gaped at him, openmouthed. She hadn't really wanted the leader's role! She'd just wanted to give Josh a hard time for stomping all over her music. But Elizabeth was giving her a big smile, Charlie was giving her a double thumbs-up, and Josh was just plain giving in.

What did I get myself into? she wondered as she accepted the instruction packet from Elizabeth. Just yesterday she was thinking of bailing, and now she was leading the team!

"When was the last time these were washed?" Jessica held up her blue Union uniform and sniffed at it suspiciously. Then she held the garment at arm's length and inspected it critically. "They're not very well cut either."

"What were you expecting?" Rob sneered as he tried on his jacket. "Southern–belle ball gowns?"

"Of course she was." Pam sniffed. "You keep forgetting Rob, that Jessica's a Theta. You know how fussy they are."

Jessica rolled her eyes at Pam's disdain. *Like you*

wouldn't give your flabby right arm to be a Theta, she thought. Ever since Pam had found out that Jessica was a member of the exclusive sorority, she'd taken every opportunity to make snide remarks about the members. It was abundantly clear to Jessica that Pam was simply green with envy.

"Mine's kind of snug," Tom complained. "The sleeves are too short. And too tight."

"Mine's *really* snug," Rob said as he struggled to do up the buttons on his jacket.

"Who cares?" Todd said as he shrugged on his own jacket and picked up his paint gun. "C'mon, we have target practice."

"Now?" Jessica exclaimed. "I wanted to hit the beach first. My tan is in serious need of attention."

"We can go later," Todd said. "Let's get done with the training first. I want to do well tomorrow."

"You guys can count on me." Rob puffed out his chest and reached for his paint gun. "I'm an excellent marksman."

With what? A slingshot? Jessica wondered as she rolled the sleeves up on her jacket.

"I'm with Todd," Neil said. "Let's get practicing." He held the door open, and everyone trooped out toward the makeshift range that had hastily been assembled on the outskirts of a parking lot. Large, black-and-white targets were lined up on the field, and Jessica could already see bright splatters of paint left behind by other competitors.

As she looked around to see how the other teams were getting on, she caught a glimpse of Elizabeth. She wasn't surprised to see that her sister was doing well, but she had to fight back laughter as Alison Quinn waltzed by, looking way more Salvation than Confederate army. Jessica smirked at the sight of Alison's bony figure swathed in a uniform ten times too big for her. "Too bad I can't shoot her right now," she muttered under her breath. Taking down Alison would make the whole trip worthwhile.

Jessica squinted through the eyepiece of her gun at the black-and-white target fifty paces away. She squeezed the trigger and whooped with joy as her bullet hit the bull's-eye. "This isn't so bad!" She smiled at Todd. "I could have fun doing this!"

"Yeah, and it will be even better tomorrow with your adrenaline pumping," Todd said as he took aim at his own target.

"I'm not really getting the hang of this," Neil said, lowering his gun. "I've missed every shot."

Jessica smirked. "Seems easy to me," she said as she fired off another bull's-eye.

"Whatever," Neil muttered. He took aim once more, but his shot went wide of the mark.

"Let me help you out," Tom offered. He walked over to Neil and stood behind him. "Line up your sights with the center of the target," he instructed. "Don't just shoot aimlessly. Take a second to focus before you pull the trigger."

"You don't have to be so scientific about it," Jessica said as she sank yet another bull's-eye. "It's totally . . . ow!" she exclaimed as one of Neil's bullets exploded on the back of her head. She wheeled around and faced him.

"Are you crazy?" she shrieked.

"It—it was an accident," Neil stammered. "I totally lost control of the gun. I'm really sorry, Jessica."

"Don't worry, Jessica," Tom assured her. "I'll work with Neil. He'll be able to shoot straight by tomorrow."

"*He* may be OK tomorrow," Jessica wailed. "But I'm going to be stuck with a bad-hair day for weeks!"

Jessica glared at Neil. As if she needed another reason to be mad at him! Not only had he outshopped her. Now he had better hair than she did too!

Sam squinted through his eyepiece in an attempt to line up the target in his sight line, but he was distracted by a sudden glimpse of blond ponytail. Elizabeth! His heart thudded against his ribs uncontrollably. He couldn't focus with her so close by. He put down his gun and grinned at the look of intense concentration on her face.

She looks so cute in that Confederate uniform, focusing so hard, he thought affectionately as he watched her sink a paint bullet in the center of the target.

And she looked so beautiful in the moonlight,

Sam remembered. And she'd felt so wonderful when he'd caught her at the edge of the cliff. He could almost feel the way her silken hair had draped across his arms and her slender yet curvaceous frame had pressed against him.

Josh clapped him on the back. "Hey, guy, what's with the goofy grin? You look a little sick."

"Or maybe just lovesick," Uli said with a smile. He joined Sam and Josh and sighted through his gun. "Hmmm," he said, peering through the eyepiece. "Let's see what Sam is focusing on. The target is not looking clear, but the view of Elizabeth is most perfect."

"Cut it out." Sam flushed as he tried to grab Uli's gun.

"I thought you were over her, buddy." Josh looked at Sam consideringly. "You dropped her like a hot potato after the county fair yesterday!"

"*Ja,* but that was after he caught her at the cliff and held her." Uli nodded knowingly.

"You guys are both being ridiculous," Sam said through clenched teeth. He picked up his gun and turned back toward the target. He concentrated fiercely on the center and was about to squeeze the trigger when Elizabeth walked across his sight line. He cursed under his breath as his shot went far afield and Josh and Uli collapsed in laughter.

"That girl's got you wrapped around her little finger," Josh said. "I don't get it. What about Angelina? In that picture you're carrying around, she looks way hotter than Wakefield. I can't imagine Elizabeth wearing a skimpy little bikini like that. She's too serious and responsible. I bet when she goes swimming, she wears one of those old-fashioned striped bathing suits. You know, the ones from the 1920s, with bloomers and stuff?"

"More important," Uli continued, "Elizabeth is messing up with your focus. How are you going to be shooting tomorrow if you don't practice now? Josh is right—maybe you should just stick with this Angelina girl. In Sweden guys go with many girls, not always just thinking about one."

"Besides," Josh said with a sly grin, "Angelina has much bigger . . ."

"Hey, guy," Sam said tightly, "watch what you're saying." For a brief second Sam wanted to punch Josh, but then Uli's words resonated in his head.

Why am I getting so hung up on one girl? he asked himself in bewilderment. Sam had an all-important rule when it came to women, and that was to keep things light and avoid entanglements. But since this stupid trip had started, he'd come dangerously close to breaking his own rule—over and over again.

He looked over to where Elizabeth stood with Ruby and Charlie. Her sweet face was serious as she showed Charlie how to sight the target. His heart fluttered for a second as he thought how nice it would be to spend the rest of the day with her. Then he looked back at Josh and Uli. Josh was grinning derisively, and Uli seemed worried.

"Did you say lovesick?" Josh said to Uli. "I think you meant love crazy."

That did it. Sam slammed his gun down on the ground. He did not like being mocked. Elizabeth Wakefield might feel great in his arms, but she was not all that. He was getting in way over his head, and he didn't like it one bit.

"C'mon, guys," Sam said. "We have the rest of the day off to sightsee, don't we?"

Uli nodded.

"Well, then, what are we waiting for?" he asked with a cocky grin. "Rumor has it that the girls in Savannah are pretty gorgeous, but I just hate to take things on faith. Let's lose these costumes and hit the town." Sam stalked off, Uli and Josh in tow, without even a backward glance at Elizabeth.

Chapter Four

"Listen, Jessica." Todd struggled to keep his voice calm. "You said this morning that you wanted to go to the beach, so what's the problem?" He watched for a minute as she attempted to comb the remains of Neil's red paint bullet out of her hair. "Besides, I bet the salt water will get the rest of the paint out."

"If three shampooings didn't do it, I doubt the ocean will," Jessica snapped. "Anyway, salt water is terrible for your hair!"

Todd rolled his eyes. *Oh, brother. Sometimes I wish she'd stayed with Elvis!*

Team One had finished their practicing and had wandered back to the Winnebago. Todd was hoping they could all do something fun together instead of hanging around the RV parking lot. He figured it made sense to try and bond the day before an event, so he'd suggested a visit to the beach.

The only problem was that nobody wanted to go.

Well, why should they? he thought with a ragged sigh as he surveyed his teammates. They were hardly the most happening group around. Jessica and Neil weren't talking to each other. Tom could barely put a sentence together without mentioning Elizabeth. And Pam and Rob and their obnoxious cooing were enough to make anybody sick.

"Look, guys, why don't we try and have a nice time together," Todd said.

"Why don't we try and have a nice time *apart*," Jessica grumbled.

"C'mon, Jess," Todd said impatiently. "I've heard the beach here is really great."

"I can't go to the beach," Pam said. "I haven't had a bikini wax in weeks."

"Thanks. That's more information than I needed to know," Todd drawled. In the past few weeks he'd grown used to hearing extremely personal details from Pam, but that didn't mean he liked it.

"Why don't we just stay here and play a spicy game of truth or dare?" Pam went on.

"No!" everyone shouted in unison.

Todd laughed as Pam's face turned an unflattering shade of tomato red. "Well, I'm glad that's one thing we all agree on!"

"I'll go to the beach if it means we don't have to play that stupid game," Neil said, getting up from his seat at the dinette table.

"I'll go to the moon if it means we don't have to play," Rob said. Strangely enough, truth or dare was one taste he and Pam did not share. Todd respected Rob for it.

"How about it, Jessica? Tom?" Todd asked as he rifled through his duffel bag for his bathing suit.

"I guess so," Tom muttered gloomily.

"If you insist." Jessica sighed.

"Hey, don't get too enthusiastic on me," Todd said sarcastically. He turned around and stared at his teammates. "In case you guys have forgotten, we're participating in a contest, and right now we're trailing everyone else. I don't know about you slackers, but I want to win the event tomorrow. We have only one more event after this one, and if we don't pull together now, we'll really be in trouble. C'mon, do you guys want to end the summer in last place with only a stupid gift certificate to show for your efforts? I just don't see any of us getting excited about buying discount kitchen and bathroom supplies," Todd went on. "I think a little team spirit is in order. We can catch a bus half a block from here that will take us right to the beach."

Todd's words seemed to whip the group into some kind of shape. Tom shrugged and grabbed his Frisbee. Neil reached for a beach towel. Rob grabbed another towel, and Pam began throwing sunblock and goggles into a tote bag. Even Jessica began to motivate, stuffing her wet hair up under a baseball cap.

Looks like we may just get some team spirit going after all, Todd thought with a wry grin as his teammates trooped out of the Winnebago. *But what* kind *of spirit is another thing altogether!*

Elizabeth wiped the paint off her fingers and threw her soldier's jacket down on her bunk with a sigh. Although she'd done very well at target practice and was looking forward to the event tomorrow, she was not in the greatest mood.

She'd certainly woken up with a smile on her face—it would have been almost impossible not to after her moonlight walk with Sam—but that was before he'd spent the morning ignoring her.

"Maybe it was just my imagination," she mused, a small frown pleating her forehead. There had been a few moments during target practice—well, more than a few moments—when Elizabeth was sure Sam was watching her every move.

Elizabeth had thought that maybe she and Sam had some kind of breakthrough the night before. He'd been kind and very romantic, in a gentlemanly sort of way. She'd even hoped they would spend some time together after practice, sight-seeing. But that was before she'd seen Sam race off with Josh and Uli.

"You look pretty down," Charlie said as she and Ruby entered the Winnebago. "What's the problem? Last time I looked, you'd hit plenty of bull's-eyes." She smiled at Elizabeth as she flopped down on her bunk.

"Yeah, we may just pull through this event," Ruby said. "Although why I care about this war reenactment thing is beyond me!"

"Yeah, maybe," Elizabeth replied shortly, silently considering how to ditch her teammates so she could go off on her own and spend some time thinking about the mess Sam was making with her life.

"Well, let's celebrate in advance, then," Charlie said. "I don't know about you guys, but I'm tired of all the junk food we've been eating. How about a fancy lunch?"

"I'm up for it," Ruby said. "If I never eat another burger again, it will be too soon."

"Well, I don't know," Elizabeth said slowly. "I kind of wanted to—"

"Real linen napkins," Charlie interrupted coaxingly.

"Flowers on every table," Ruby said. "And fresh lemonade, not out of a can."

"Maybe some French pastries," Charlie added with a gleam in her eye. "We could even get a little dressed up."

Elizabeth threw back her head and laughed. "OK, guys, you win." She was touched that Charlie and Ruby wanted to include her in their outing, and she couldn't help remembering the beginning of the trip. Back then the three girls had a hard time just being civil to each other. They certainly hadn't wanted to hang together.

"Any ideas where we should go?" she asked.

"I've heard the historic district has some nice places to eat," Charlie said, reaching for an embroidered blouse and shrugging out of her T-shirt.

"Yeah, it's supposed to be the place to see," Ruby chimed in as she pulled her wild mane of curls into a high ponytail.

"Sounds good to me." Elizabeth stepped out of her chinos and took a pair of linen pants out of her duffel. She pulled them up over her slim legs and grabbed her purse from the bed. "Let's get going!"

It was only about half a mile to the historic district, and Elizabeth felt her spirits begin to lift as she took in the beautiful Federal architecture of the public squares. Elegant antebellum houses clustered around ornate fountains, and old-fashioned horse-drawn carriages showing tourists the city passed them by.

"This is gorgeous." Charlie sighed wistfully. "I wish Scott was here. I'd love to take one of those carriage rides with him."

I wouldn't mind taking one with Sam either, Elizabeth thought. *But somehow I don't think that's going to happen.* Her sigh echoed Charlie's.

"OK, girl, spill," Ruby demanded.

"What do you mean?" Elizabeth asked innocently

as they stopped in front of a fancy outdoor café. "Hey, this looks good. What do you think?" She gestured at the pretty round tables that were shaded by a gaily striped awning.

"I think you're avoiding my question," Ruby said with a laugh as she seated herself in one of the cane chairs. "You look pretty down. What's going on?"

"Guy trouble?" Charlie said in her soft voice.

Elizabeth avoided Charlie's sympathetic gaze and fiddled with the vase of tea roses that graced the table. She was a little unsure of what to say.

"I think it's more Sam trouble than just guy trouble," Ruby said perceptively as she flipped open her menu. "There's that weird vibe going on between you."

"Is it that obvious?" Elizabeth asked with a worried frown. Her two friends burst out laughing.

"Oh yeah. There's some major tension whenever you two are within five feet of each other," Charlie said, leaning forward and putting her elbows on the table. "When he caught you at Lookout Mountain yesterday, I thought he was going into nice-Sam stage."

Elizabeth smiled slightly.

"Nice Sam? I used to think there was something more to Sam than his obnoxious side, but now I'm not so sure. That guy's not real. No normal person swings from being polite to being a total jerk if he's *really* nice," Ruby said sarcastically.

"Nasty Sam is more like it. Did you hear how Sam was going on with Josh afterward? They make me sick." Ruby's frown turned to a smile when the waitress appeared at her elbow. "Guys, what do you want?"

"Chicken salad and iced tea," Charlie ordered.

"Make that two," Ruby said.

"Make it three," Elizabeth said absently as she mulled over Ruby's words.

"So, tell us what's wrong," Charlie said eagerly after the waitress had returned with tall, mint-sprigged glasses of iced tea.

"I don't really know what there is to tell." Elizabeth took a sip of her tea. "At the beginning of the trip I couldn't stand him. You saw the way he behaved. He was horrible to everyone."

"Yeah." Ruby nodded. "The guy has major attitude."

"But there's more to him than attitude," Elizabeth said quickly.

"He is cute," Charlie admitted. "In a scruffy kind of way. And smart."

"And I really like him. At least, I think I do." Elizabeth frowned as a plate of chicken salad was placed in front of her. She picked up her fork. "Last night while everybody was sleeping, the Winnebago ran out of gas. Sam and I went to buy some from a gas station we'd passed about a mile back."

"Let me guess," Charlie said, swallowing a bite

of chicken salad. "It was all moonlight and magic, right?" She nodded when she saw the look of admission on Elizabeth's face. "I say you should follow your heart. If you want Sam, go after him. Don't worry so much that he runs hot and cold. Guys do that. He'll come around. You have to remember that love is the most important thing."

"I say forget him," Ruby said emphatically. "He's totally thoughtless. Besides, why load yourself down with emotional commitments? Don't you want to focus on your own life? The most important thing isn't love. It's figuring out what you want to do and going for it. Not wasting energy on some guy who treats you like dirt."

Elizabeth looked between the girls with a small smile. She'd never really had a heart-to-heart conversation with anyone like Charlie or Ruby before the ICSN Coast-to-Coast road trip. Back in high school her best friend, Enid Rollins, had been as serious and studious as she was. Her best friend at SVU, Nina Harper, was so hardworking and responsible that she made Elizabeth feel like a slacker. She certainly never thought she'd be eagerly taking advice from one girl who was unmarried and pregnant and another one whose dream was to quit school and hit the road as a singer. But as different as Ruby's and Charlie's dreams were from her own, Elizabeth admired their gutsiness. In some ways they seemed so much more mature than she did.

After all, Elizabeth asked herself as she picked at her chicken salad, would she be as brave as Charlie in the face of an unplanned pregnancy? Would she be able to stay as focused as Ruby was on a difficult dream?

"Well," Ruby prodded. "What do you think?"

"I don't know what I think," Elizabeth said slowly. *No, that's wrong,* she told herself. *I think that you both have a lot more on the ball than I realized. And I think that I'm more confused about Sam than ever!*

"I got it!" Neil yelled as he leaped through the sparkling surf and caught the bright yellow Frisbee in midair. He threw the Frisbee to Tom.

"You have a great throwing arm," Tom commented as he tossed the Frisbee to Todd. "Have you ever gone out for baseball?"

"Nah." Neil shook his head. "I was never really into organized sports." He caught the Frisbee easily as Todd sent it back his way and, giving it a little spin, threw it toward Rob.

"Hey, what about me?" Pam complained as Rob tossed the Frisbee to Jessica.

"Sorry, babe." Rob shrugged. His eyes had nearly popped out of his head at the sight of Jessica in her tiny blue bikini, and now there was a little friction in the air between him and Pam.

But in spite of Rob and Pam's latest spat, and even though Jessica was pointedly ignoring him,

Neil realized the team was having a great time and getting along better than it had in ages.

Jessica caught the Frisbee and held it in her hands for a second. "Hmmm," she said, "who should I throw this to?" She tilted her head and looked around the circle.

Neil regarded her uncertainly. She was standing directly across from him in the water, and the logical thing would be for her to toss the Frisbee to him.

But that doesn't mean she will, Neil thought regretfully. It was hard for him to stay mad at Jessica when they were all having such fun splashing through the waves, but it was obvious that Jessica wasn't having a hard time staying mad at him.

If only he hadn't splattered her hair. Neil sighed. He could understand why she was angry about that, but she had to have forgiven him for the shopping incident already. Right? Neil held his breath as he waited for Jessica to throw the Frisbee.

"Catch," Jessica called gleefully. She sent the yellow disk flying toward Pam.

Pam lunged through the waves and grabbed the Frisbee just before it sank to the bottom. "Here you go, snookums," she cried as she tossed it to Rob.

"I'm over Frisbee," Todd announced. "Who wants to swim out to that buoy over there?" He pointed to a bright orange buoy about a quarter mile out, bobbing gently in the waves.

"I'm up for it!" Tom dove into the water.

"Whoever gets there first wins a free round tonight!" Todd cried as he struck out after Tom.

"In that case, you guys better get ready to open your wallets," Rob yelled as he plunged in after them.

Neil had to smile at the sight of pudgy Rob trying to outdistance Tom and Todd. Both Watts and Wilkins were superbly conditioned.

"What about you?" Pam asked Neil. "Aren't you going to show us what a macho man you are?"

Neil swallowed hard. Pam's comment had left Jessica with another perfect opening to spill his secret. So far, he was pretty sure Jessica hadn't told anyone that he was gay—at least, she'd kept her mouth shut in Chicago—but that didn't mean she wouldn't do it now.

But Jessica just tossed her golden hair and walked by him toward the beach. "I'm going to catch some rays," she announced.

"I think I'll wait here for Rob," Pam simpered. "He'll need a victory hug when he comes back."

"Yeah, whatever." Neil shrugged as he watched Jessica lay her towel out on the sand. He thought again about the fact that although Jessica had had plenty of opportunities to spill his secret—including a chance to blab on live TV!—she'd kept her mouth shut.

Does that mean that deep down she really does want to make up? Neil wondered as he waded toward the shore. The fact that she had kept his secret meant a great deal to him. He wasn't quite ready to come out. And now he realized that he could really trust Jessica.

Maybe she's just waiting for me to apologize. Maybe she's still a little burned or embarrassed from when I reamed her out in front of everybody after the Opry event. Neil frowned as he walked along the sand to where Jessica was sitting on a pink-and-white-striped beach towel. It might be his turn to make a peace offering, he realized. He stopped in front of Jessica's towel and smiled down at her.

Jessica was rifling through her bag and didn't notice him. He watched as she pulled a tube of sunblock out of her bag and unscrewed the cap.

"Let me help you with that," Neil offered. He pumped some false bravado into his voice as he took the tube out of her hand. "I can reach your back better than you can."

Jessica looked up at Neil for the first time and recoiled. She gaped at him as if he had suggested that she strip naked and fling herself at the first passing guy. With a muttered curse she grabbed her bag and her towel and scampered off down the beach.

So much for a peace offering, Neil thought sadly. Nobody had looked at him with such disgust since the third grade, when he'd put a frog down Darcy Grant's shirt. He tried to make light of the moment, but his heart was heavy as he wandered back to the water.

Homophobic, he thought as he plunged into the surf. *Jessica hates me because I'm gay.*

Chapter
Five

Elizabeth adjusted the jacket of her uniform and made her way over to where her team was waiting in the specially roped-off area of Skidaway Island State Park. Along the way she narrowly avoided being sideswiped by an ICSN camera tech snaking cable through the grass.

The ICSN crew were out in full force to tape the event. Sponsors and announcers were racing back and forth, trying to get sound bites from the various competitors. Elizabeth had no interest in giving her thoughts on the Civil War reenactment, but she wasn't surprised to see Ruby and Josh being interviewed by Ned Jackson, the ICSN head field producer, for the Coast-to-Coast *Real Notes* show. After all, Ruby insisted that she had only come on the road trip to get the publicity she needed to launch her singing career, and Josh . . . Well, Josh was just vain. He needed to have people pay attention to him.

"Are you nervous?" Charlie asked timidly as Elizabeth fought her way past the crowds to join her.

"A little," Elizabeth admitted. "I actually didn't care so much when we were in last place, but now we have something to lose."

"*Ja,*" Uli said, shifting his paint gun from hand to hand. "I am feeling the same way."

"I know what you mean," Ruby said as she and Josh joined them. She slung her paint gun over her shoulder. "I feel like a lot is riding on this event, especially since I'm playing general."

"Hey, you asked for it." Josh shrugged. "What about you, Sam? Ready?"

"Sure," Sam said. "What about the rest of you?"

Elizabeth couldn't help but notice that Sam avoided her eyes. She hoped that his feelings for her—whatever they were—didn't screw up the event for their team.

"I think that—" Ruby was interrupted by Richie Valentine, speaking into a microphone from a small platform outside one of the ICSN vans. He wore a bright yellow T-shirt plastered all over with the names of the various sponsors and a big, TV-personality smile.

"Listen up, teams, 'cause I know you're all just raring to get out there and fight the good fight." Elizabeth rolled her eyes. "But war isn't pretty, folks, so you'd better be prepared. Follow your generals, and be prepared to shed some paint. The team that suffers the least casualties and manages to take the most prisoners or kill the most enemies wins."

"OK, guys," Ruby said as Team Two looked back at her. "Here's the plan. Elizabeth, you be the front line. Go out there and try and hit as many Union soldiers as possible. They're hidden in the trees right now, but the moment they see us, they're going to come out shooting. Sam, you cover Elizabeth. I want you two to clear a path for Josh and me to go in and take prisoners. Charlie and Uli, you bring up the rear. Everybody clear?"

Sam smirked, and Josh mumbled something about Ruby's plan being stupid. Elizabeth and Charlie nodded. Elizabeth couldn't help but wonder what Sam really thought about having to cover her. Had Ruby chosen Sam because she thought their working together would help them overcome their difficulties? She flashed Ruby a quizzical glance, but it was clear that Ruby's attention was focused on more than her teammates' personal communication problems.

"OK, guys, let's do it," Ruby said firmly. She led the team over to a thin, red line chalked on the grass. Team Two assembled behind it alongside Team Three, and Elizabeth caught a brief glimpse of Alison Quinn holding her paint gun the wrong way around. She knew that Teams One and Four were lying in wait, and her heart began to beat faster.

"Are you ready?" Richie Valentine held the starter gun high in the air. "Let's go!" *Bang!*

The gun exploded with a loud pop, and Elizabeth ran forward in a semicrouch, her gun in attack position, her eyes darting left and right, on the lookout for the enemy. Adrenaline was pumping through her veins, and her senses were superalert. A flash of blue caught her eye, and she saw Mickey James from Team Four snake his way out from behind one of the trees.

Elizabeth felt a moment of fear as she found herself looking down the front of his gun barrel. But her reflexes were lightning quick, and while Mickey was still struggling to line her up in his sights, she fired off her gun. Suddenly the front of Mickey's uniform was splattered with bright green paint.

"I got you!" Elizabeth whooped joyfully. Then she whirled around just in time to see Eric Nyberg, also from Team Four, aiming his gun at her.

"No, please!" Elizabeth dropped to her knees. "Don't shoot! You'll get paint all over my face at this range," she pleaded. "Take me prisoner instead."

"Less points if I do." Eric grinned and raised his gun.

"Take that!" Elizabeth cried as she fired off a round. Eric gaped in surprise as he looked down at his chest, covered in green paint.

"That was pretty tricky," he said admiringly.

"You'd better lie down. You're dead, you know," Elizabeth said as she got to her knees. She was feeling extra cocky after scoring two hits in her first five minutes. In a crouch she began moving toward a clump of bushes. She was sure that she could see a blue uniform peeking out between the leaves.

"Ow!" Elizabeth cried out as she tumbled to the ground. She groaned and glared accusingly at the twisted root that had managed to trip her up. The Union army hadn't gotten her. A stupid branch had!

"Elizabeth's down!" Sam yelled, although he knew that no one from his team would be able to hear him over the gunfire.

Forget the gunfire. They wouldn't be able to hear me over the beating of my own heart! His face was white with fear, and his mouth was set in a grim line. Sam wasn't afraid of a few paint bullets, but he was terrified that Elizabeth had been genuinely hurt. The expression of pain on her face when she turned onto her back made his stomach churn.

Sam didn't care if he was hit. His one objective was to cover Elizabeth from any more hostile fire and drag her away from the enemy lines.

He dashed forward, eluding the bullets that whizzed by his ear, and flung himself on top of Elizabeth. Her body was soft and yielding underneath his, and all thoughts of the battle that was raging around them disappeared as he looked into her eyes.

She's so incredible, Sam thought. He could feel Elizabeth's warm breath across his cheek, and he had an almost overwhelming desire to kiss her. She squirmed underneath him, sending shivers of delight through his body.

"I've got you covered," he whispered in her ear. "You're safe now."

"I was safe before!" Elizabeth hissed. She struggled to a sitting position and tried to push him away, but Sam's hold on her was too strong for her to disentangle herself completely. Finally she got up on her knees, although Sam's arms were still clasped around her.

"What are you doing, Sam?" she demanded, her eyes flashing fire. "This isn't what Ruby meant when she said you were supposed to cover me!"

Sam stared at her. He was too stunned by her outburst to reply, but he didn't need to because Elizabeth continued to rage at him.

"What do you think, that I'm some kind of weak little damsel in distress? In case you hadn't noticed, I'm a soldier, a good soldier, and there's a war going on! Let me fight it, OK?"

"I don't believe it!" Tom exclaimed from his hiding place in the bushes. He parted the leaves in order to get a better look.

"Sam Burgess has got to be the slimiest guy on the planet! He picks the middle of a battle to jump Elizabeth!" Tom's voice was so thick with rage, he was practically growling. *And how dare he beat me to it!* he added silently.

Tom was so outraged by the sight of Elizabeth entangled in Sam's arms that he was completely paralyzed. "He's practically groveling at her feet!" he muttered darkly.

"Psst!"

Tom jumped in fright and whirled around, his gun at the ready. It was Todd. He lowered his gun and sagged against the bush in relief. "What are you doing? Trying to frighten me to death?"

"I'm trying to fight a battle," Todd hissed. "What are *you* doing?"

"I'm staking out the enemy," Tom replied stiffly. "I've practically got Elizabeth and that Burgess creep in a missile lock. Go find your own soldiers to shoot, and don't waste time checking up on me."

"Sam and Elizabeth are dead," Todd said, peering through the leafy branches.

"What?" Tom parted the branches and thrust

his entire head through the bush, completely oblivious to the paint bullets that were exploding inches away from him.

"They were fine just a minute ago!" he wailed.

"Take cover!" Todd grabbed the edge of Tom's jacket and pulled him back into the underbrush. "Listen, Tom, don't give me some lame story about how you were about to shoot her. I know what you were doing, and spying on Elizabeth is not the way to win her heart. You want to capture her attention? Win this thing!"

"You're right!" Tom said. *I've got to prove to Elizabeth that I'm more of a man than Sam Burgess!*

"Cover me. I'm going in," he said with determination. He cocked his gun and took off.

Jessica inched along the ground in a belly crawl. The butt of her rifle poked uncomfortably against her ribs, but she didn't even care. Her mind was totally focused on one thing. Wasting Alison Quinn.

Unfortunately Alison was proving to be a slippery target. Who knew those bony hips would be so perfect for sliding through the underbrush? Jessica grumbled as Alison squeezed herself underneath a small cropping of bushes.

"Darn!" Jessica cried. Even though Alison had managed to evade her, she refused to give up. Jessica was determined to shed some paint. She loved the excitement of the battle. The sound of the bullets flying and the sight of the splattered paint that dotted the ground spurred her on.

I've got to find a target, she thought as she crouched and held the rifle to her eye. Any Southern soldier within a fifty-yard range would do.

Got one! She held her rifle steady as Cynthia Lewis from Team Three came within her sights. "Steady now, steady . . . ," Jessica murmured as her fingers tightened on the trigger.

The sound of a twig crunching alerted her, and she spun around just in time to see Trey Green, also from Team Three, grinning at her from behind his rifle. Trey fired off a shot, and Jessica saw a bullet explode in a splatter of yellow paint on a low-hanging branch, just inches from her shoulder. Acting on sheer instinct, Jessica went into a drop and roll. The bumpy ground bruised her, but she didn't care as she tumbled down the slight incline and into a pile of branches. The branches broke her fall, and she nimbly jumped up and crouched behind them.

Awesome! Jessica was ecstatic. She'd managed to elude capture, and she'd landed in a perfect lookout spot. She stooped and grabbed a handful of dirt. If Lila could see her now . . . She grinned and rubbed the dirt against her cheeks in a crude attempt at camouflage.

Another Confederate! Jessica recognized Charlie, from Team Two, just coming into her sights. This time she was going to get her soldier. Jessica raised her gun and prepared to fire, but no sooner had she let fly with a bullet than Ruby, like an avenging angel, appeared out of nowhere and dropped to the ground, taking Charlie with her. Jessica's bullet sailed cleanly through the air where Charlie's head had been two seconds earlier and splattered in a burst of red against the trunk of a tree.

I've got to hit someone! she told herself in frustration. *It's not fair!*

Out of the corner of her eye Jessica saw a movement in the leafy underbrush a hundred paces to her right. She went very still, hardly daring to breathe.

"OK, this is the one," she whispered as she brought her gun up to her shoulder. Take aim and . . . It was Neil! Her shoulders sagged in disappointment as she realized that she had been about to hit one of her teammates.

Well, why not? Jessica was itching to hit something, and as far as she knew, while hitting a fellow teammate wouldn't win her any points, it wouldn't lose her any either.

"Let's see how you like getting paint in *your* hair," Jessica muttered as she set her sights on

Neil's tall, broad-shouldered frame and let fly with a bright red bullet.

What a team! Todd shook his head in disbelief. How were they ever going to pull themselves out of last place? He watched in amazement as Jessica splattered Neil with bullets. Didn't she know that Neil was on her own side?

"Team! That's a laugh!" Todd snorted sarcastically. At least Tom had whipped himself into shape after their little talk, and Todd had been satisfied to see him waste Josh Margolin of Team Two.

Todd dropped to a crouch and scurried behind a large clump of brush. He needed to take a breather after the almost constant running and shooting of the past half hour. So far he'd managed to escape capture, but he hadn't been able to splatter anybody. He'd had his sights on Team Three's Murph Roberts and had been about to fire off a shot when Murph had dashed behind a tree—managing to shoot Pam as he did so.

I'm glad Rob got him, Todd thought as he darted his head out from behind the brush, searching for likely targets. For someone built like the Pillsbury Doughboy, Rob was doing pretty well. *Better than the rest of us anyway,* he thought.

Todd heard a war whoop and turned to see Danny Wyatt of Team Four doing a victory dance over the paint-splattered body of Team Three's Tina Albert. "Looks like Team Four's doing OK," Todd muttered, but it was Team Three who was really clearing the battlefield.

Todd stiffened as he heard the sound of branches being trampled and whipped around. Just a squirrel. He managed to laugh, but his heart was in his throat. *I'd better get out here,* he chided himself. *C'mon, Wilkins, enough sitting around.* Todd left the safety of the brush and, running low to the ground, hurled himself into the heat of the battle.

His team might be losing, but he wasn't going to go down without a fight.

"I could have shot a lot more people." Elizabeth scowled. She crossed her arms over her chest and stared defiantly at Ruby and Charlie, who were sitting across from her at the wooden, picnic-style table.

The event had ended hours ago, and the girls had decided to head down to the waterfront area and eat in one of the River Street pubs. Ruby and Charlie were interested in seeing some local color, and the area certainly provided plenty of that. Local bands were giving impromptu concerts, and Ruby had sung along with one of them for a few tunes. Crowds of college students spilled out of the cafés and onto the wharf, and local craftspeople sold their pottery and jewelry from squares of colorful fabric spread on the ground.

"I was doing really well," she continued as she toyed with her glass of root beer. "I took out Eric Nyberg and Mickey James. I'd like to have seen Sam do that. If he hadn't gotten us killed, I bet Team Two wouldn't have come in second." She had been so sure they were going to wipe the field. She had been off to such a great start!

But Elizabeth and Uli had been the only members of Team Two to shoot anybody. Sam might have thought that he was protecting Elizabeth, but his intervention had cost them their lives when Briana Fulton of Team Four had managed to hit them both with one bullet.

Team Three had led the pack, scoring big time and pulling up from third to second place with an overall score of 180. Team Four had somehow managed to do worse than Team Two, placing last and moving into third place behind Team Three with an overall score of 150. Team One, while still in last place overall, had managed to come in third, thanks in part to Tom Watts totally wasting Josh and Rob managing to inflict several casualties on Team Four.

"You did a great job," Charlie said soothingly. "Much better than I did. I didn't get anyone, and I would have been creamed by your sister if Ruby hadn't saved me."

"Something tells me that our Miss Elizabeth

isn't really upset about losing." Ruby gave Elizabeth a shrewd look. "I mean, we're still in first place overall. No, I think what's really getting her is that Sam stopped her."

"You're right." Elizabeth nodded. "I can't stand the way he acted, like he thought I was some kind of incompetent female." She shook her head in disgust and dug into the basket of potato chips that was in the center of the table. "Anyone could see that I'd just tripped over a stupid branch. Did he think that I wouldn't be able to stand up on my own?"

"I don't think that was it at all," Charlie said thoughtfully. "I think Sam thought you were really hurt. Sam likes to act as if nothing gets to him, but I think *you* really get to him, Elizabeth. The problem is he doesn't know how to show his feelings except when he thinks you're in trouble."

Elizabeth frowned as Charlie's words sank in. Could Charlie be right?

"What I want to know is *how* he felt," Ruby said with a wicked grin. "I was about two hundred yards behind you, and I could practically see the steam rising out of the ground. Let me tell you, girl, it looked hot."

It felt hot too, Elizabeth thought, and blushed furiously. As mad as she was at Sam, she couldn't deny that the way his body had lain across hers had been extremely sexy. "It was . . . OK," she murmured bashfully.

"OK?" Ruby hooted with laughter. She leaned forward, her brown eyes sparkling in amusement. "Your face just turned fire-engine red because it felt *OK*? I mean, I might not like the guy, but even I can admit Sam's a babe."

Charlie giggled as Elizabeth's face turned an even more fiery shade of crimson. "I think you're just as confused about Sam as he is about you. Look, Elizabeth, why don't we all just forget about the contest and . . . everything else for a while," Charlie said kindly.

"We could do some sight-seeing." Ruby reached into her purse and pulled out a guide-book.

"Our time in Savannah is up, though," Elizabeth reminded her. "We have to get down to Miami and catch the prop planes to Key West."

"Who says we can't have a little fun along the way?" Ruby asked, wrinkling her forehead in concentration as she flipped through her guide-book.

"I think it's a great idea," Charlie enthused. "I know we've traveled across the country, but I feel like we haven't seen much of anything. Except for the event stops. I'd really like to go slow for these next couple of days and . . ."

"I think it's a lousy idea."

Elizabeth whipped up her head, and Ruby and Charlie turned around in surprise. Sam and Josh were standing by their table.

113

"Of all the places in this town, they had to find ours," Elizabeth muttered unhappily.

It was clear from the dark expression on Sam's face and the beer he held in his hand that he'd been drinking. It was also clear that he was furious about Team Two coming in second.

"We don't have time to waste," he said tightly. "We have to book if we want to make it down to Miami in time to catch the plane." He tilted back his head and drained his beer.

"Yeah," Josh added with a nasty sneer. "After someone screwed up today, we can't risk missing the last event."

"Excuse me?" Elizabeth spluttered. "Are you insinuating that it was *my* fault we didn't win?"

"You bet it was." Sam's eyes flickered over to her. "If you hadn't been so clumsy, I wouldn't have had to risk both our lives trying to help you."

"Help me?" Elizabeth stared at him in disbelief. "*You* were the one who got us both killed!"

"Yeah, right. Will you listen to her?" Sam turned to Josh. "Can you believe the stuff she's spilling? Listen, Elizabeth, I don't care what you say to make yourself feel better. The point is, we'd better be on that tarmac in Miami tomorrow evening. Remember, we barely made it to Wall, South Dakota, in time for that event."

"Yeah," Ruby snapped. "And that turned out to be our lucky break, didn't it? If we hadn't

114

been so late, we would already have downed all the ice water, like everyone on Teams One, Three, and Four."

"Look, you know that if we're late for that plane, we're automatically disqualified," Sam shot back.

Elizabeth was dimly aware that Ruby fired off an equally sharp rejoinder, but she wasn't really listening.

Charlie was wrong. Elizabeth's mouth twisted in a bitter smile. She wasn't confused about Sam. She knew exactly how she felt about him. He was selfish, overbearing, argumentative, and nasty. And right then, she didn't care if she never saw him again!

Chapter
Six

"Hey, guy, just think. In less than twenty-four hours you'll be in the arms of that babe. She is *so* hot! Does she have any friends?" Josh quirked an eyebrow at Sam as he raised his glass of virgin sangria to his lips.

"I don't know," Sam replied shortly. He was still smarting from the way Elizabeth had reamed him out during the event the day before, and not even the thought of Angelina in her teeny-tiny bikini could lift the black cloud that hung over his head.

The mood in the Winnebago as they'd driven through Georgia and on into Florida had been about as peaceful as the re-creation of the Civil War battle. Elizabeth hadn't spoken two words to him the whole night. She, Ruby, and Charlie had huddled together at the back of the Winnebago as if he and the other two guys were carrying a deadly virus. He'd figured that she'd get over her bad mood after a good night's sleep, but the morning hadn't brought any improvement.

He glanced over at the white wicker table where she sat with Ruby and Charlie. They'd stopped at a small outdoor restaurant on Magnolia Avenue in St. Augustine to refuel and stretch their legs. The avenue was supposed to be one of the prettiest streets in America, and the Spanish-style café they'd chosen definitely supported that claim. Sam glanced around at the bougainvillea-draped arbor and the gaily striped umbrellas that shielded each table. He thought that being in such a charming spot might help to finally bring Elizabeth around, but so far that didn't seem to be the case either.

So what? Who cares? Sam said to himself. *Elizabeth Wakefield is not your concern!*

"Your drink, it's OK?" Uli looked at Sam questioningly. "You had a most bad expression on your face just now. I'm thinking maybe the drink is not sweet enough?"

"It's plenty sweet," Sam said gruffly. He drained his glass in a single swallow. "I'm just upset about the contest." He looked away from Uli.

"Ja." Uli nodded. "We could have done much better yesterday, but we are still in first place, no?"

"So what?" Josh frowned. "We're only leading by a couple of points. The balance could tip real easily. Who knows what we're supposed to do in

Key West? Maybe it won't be so easy. Maybe we're supposed to go deep-sea diving and land a shark or something."

"Land a shark?" Uli questioned.

"It's an expression," Sam explained. "'Land' means to catch. Josh is worried we might have to catch some pretty big fish."

"But that should be easy." Uli's brow cleared. "In Sweden, I am often fishing for salmon. But why do you say we will be fishing?"

"Just a hunch." Josh shrugged. "Think about it. Each event had something to do with the location where the event took place." He ticked off the events on his fingers. "In Vegas we hit the casinos. In Twin Falls it was white-water rafting. In South Dakota we tried to cool off with ice water. In St. Joseph it was the Pony Express. In Chicago, baseball. Yesterday in Savannah we played the North against the South. Now, what else do they do in Key West besides fish?"

Sam shrugged. Josh's chatter was taking his mind off Elizabeth. A little. "You know what I think?" he said. "I think we've already been through enough hairy stuff. Key West is the end of the line, the last event, and ICSN is probably going to give us a break. We might be fishing, sure," he said to Josh. "But it won't be any strenuous, deep-sea stuff. We'll probably hang out on a pleasure boat all day, catch some rays, and see which team can land the most minnows or something."

"You know, you're probably right." Josh grinned. "That would be sweet. It'll be sweetest for you, though," he added, elbowing Sam in the ribs. "You'll probably *need* to kick back and relax with a fishing rod and a can of beer. I bet you're going to have a wild night with Angelina. When are you going to call her?"

Sam rubbed his unshaven cheek and considered. For a long time now he hadn't been that excited about hooking up with his ex. He absolutely refused to believe it was because Elizabeth Wakefield had gotten under his skin.

He looked at Elizabeth. She was poring over a map, and her brow was knitted in fierce concentration. In her crisp white pants and green-and-white-checked blouse she looked about as wild as a kindergarten teacher. Sam reached in the pocket of his cargo pants for the photo of Angelina he'd taken to carrying. There was no denying that she was one sexy redhead. He glanced back at Elizabeth as Uli whistled and grabbed the photo.

Why am I even hesitating? he asked himself. Why was he even wasting time thinking about someone as straitlaced as Elizabeth Wakefield?

"You are going to be having a lot of fun when we are in Florida," Uli said, his eyes bulging as he studied Angelina's generous curves.

"That's right." Sam nodded as he took back and pocketed the picture. He'd made his decision. As soon as he hit the Keys, he was racing to the nearest phone and making a date with a girl he knew could show him a good time. "I *will* be having a lot of fun." He poured himself another glass of sangria from the pitcher on the table and raised it in a toast.

Ruby finished singing, and the last notes of the soulful ballad she'd written floated out on the gentle summer breeze. She bowed slightly as Elizabeth and Charlie clapped. "Thanks, guys," she said with a smile. She took a sip of her lemonade and looked at Elizabeth, poring over a map.

"Thinking of anyplace special?" she asked.

"How about Cape Canaveral?" Elizabeth pointed at a spot on the map with her finger.

Cape Canaveral? Ruby couldn't help smiling. She'd come to respect Elizabeth over the past few weeks, but some things about the girl she'd never understand. The road to Miami was filled with wild places to stop—Daytona Beach, Palm Beach, Fort Lauderdale. But Cape Canaveral? What was there besides NASA?

"Are you sure you want to stop in Cape Canaveral?" Ruby asked.

"Why not?" Elizabeth glanced up from the map. "We're making good time, no matter what Sam thinks. We can definitely fit in another stop before we have to be in Miami."

"I know that," Ruby said. "I meant, don't you want to stop somewhere fun?"

121

"Cape Canaveral will be fun!" Elizabeth protested. "We can visit the Kennedy Space Center too."

"Oh, sure." Charlie smiled, and Ruby rolled her eyes. "If you're interested in hearing a lecture on the shuttle program," Charlie said. "C'mon, Elizabeth, it's a gorgeous day. Wouldn't you rather go to the beach? I say we push forward and make it to Daytona Beach."

"Forget the beach." Ruby put down her guitar and reached into her pocket for a rubber band. She gathered her hair into a ponytail and snapped the rubber band around it. "I say we hit the track!"

"The track?" Elizabeth frowned. "What do you mean? Like for horses?"

"No, the *racetrack*. You know, fast cars, cute guys, plenty of heart-stopping action." Ruby's eyes sparkled in anticipation.

"The racetrack!" Charlie squealed. "That sounds so, so . . ."

"So dangerous," Elizabeth finished for her. "I don't think so, Ruby."

"Oh, c'mon. Is this the girl who was so mad because she only got a chance to waste two people yesterday? Where's your spirit, Elizabeth? And just when I thought you were beginning to show a little backbone."

"It just sounds too wild, Ruby." Elizabeth shrugged. "The racetrack in Daytona is world famous. I'm not—"

Ruby groaned. "Not the professional track! There's an amateur track where we can actually drive the cars. Just think of how fun it will be." She paused for a second and dropped her voice. "Just think what Sam will say!"

"What do you mean, 'what Sam will say'? And anyway, who cares?" Elizabeth knit her brow in an angry frown.

"I guess you're right," Ruby said innocently. "It's just that you seemed so mad yesterday when you thought Sam was treating you like a weak, incompetent woman." She shrugged. "I just thought that if he knew you were whipping around a racetrack in a little red hot rod, he might, you know, get a different idea about you."

"Well, all right," Elizabeth said slowly after a moment. "Who knows? It might be really fun!"

I knew that would get her! Ruby bit her lip to keep from laughing and winked at Charlie. "Daytona, here we come!"

"I've been dying to stretch my legs for the past four hours!" Todd moaned in relief as he got out of the driver's seat and climbed out of the Winnebago.

"I know what you mean." Jessica massaged her own shoulders and stretched tall. Then she smiled as she looked around the roadside café. "Oh my gosh! There's Team Two! What a coincidence!"

"Let's hope they were just leaving," Tom

muttered as he leaped out of the Winnebago and joined Todd and Jessica on the pavement.

And let's hope Watts doesn't pick a fight with Burgess or do something else equally stupid, Todd thought as he looked at Tom. It was clear from the expression on Watts's face that the sight of Sam Burgess did not make him happy.

"I'm thirsty," Rob wailed.

"So am I, Robbie-pie," Pam cooed. "Why don't you go get us some iced teas and we can sit at one of these adorable little tables."

"I'm going to say hi to Elizabeth," Jessica announced. "See you guys in a few."

"What are you in the mood for?" Tom asked Todd.

"I think I'll just grab a soda and walk around for a few minutes," Todd said. "I need a little exercise."

Todd walked into the café and ordered. He closed his eyes as the icy-cold soda slid down his throat. *Man, I needed that,* he thought as he put down his empty glass and walked outside again into the bright sunshine. Jessica was sitting with Elizabeth and the other girls from Team Two. Rob and Pam appeared to be giving each other artificial respiration. Gross. And Tom was parked at a table by himself, looking daggers at Sam, who sat with Josh and Uli at a table near the back of the outdoor patio area.

For a moment Todd wondered if he should

join his teammate. Bad idea. He was starting to feel as if he and Tom were joined at the hip.

Todd surveyed the small, well-kept outdoor café appreciatively. A trellis groaned under the weight of a mass of oleander and bougainvillea. Todd decided to take a look behind the trellis, at the field of wildflowers that seemed to spread for miles.

Todd circled the trellis and sniffed the sweet flowers. The scene would have been totally peaceful if it weren't for the fact that suddenly he could hear everything Sam, Josh, and Uli were saying. *Their table must be just on the other side of the trellis,* Todd realized.

Not that they have anything interesting to say, he thought as he heard Uli explaining the merits of different kinds of fish bait. Todd was just about to walk back to the café for another soda when Sam's voice made him stop in his tracks.

"You're so right, man. I'm going to have a seriously good time with her."

Todd hesitated. Was Sam talking about Elizabeth? And then he got angry. Just who did Burgess think he was anyway? Todd parted the bougainvillea and peered through the arbor. Sam's back was to him.

"She has an amazing body." Josh, sitting next to Sam, was shaking his head over a small, crumpled picture. Todd could just barely make out that the picture was of a particularly well-built redhead.

Put your eyes back in your head, boy, Todd thought, looking at Josh in disgust. *You're practically drooling.*

"Why you've been wasting time with Wakefield when you have this chick lined up is beyond me," Josh continued.

"I'm not wasting my time with Wakefield. Not anymore," Sam said firmly.

As if Elizabeth isn't worth twelve of you, Burgess! Todd fumed. He couldn't get over the garbage he was hearing. Even though Todd and Elizabeth were no longer going out, he still loved her. He always would. How could he not? He'd known her for practically his whole life, and he couldn't bear the thought of pond scum like Burgess messing with her head.

Well, he won't get a chance to. Not if I have anything to say about it, Todd vowed as his hands curled into fists. He had to keep Burgess away from Elizabeth. Had to stop Burgess from leading Elizabeth on and then throwing her away—again.

Todd turned to leave. He'd heard all he needed to hear. Now he needed to . . . "Ow!"

He slammed into Tom's chest.

"What are you doing, Watts?" he demanded. "Were you standing right behind me the whole time? Why don't you try for real closeness? Want a piggyback ride back to the Winnebago?"

"Never mind that now," Tom whispered impatiently. "Did you hear what that lowlife was saying?

What are we going to do about it?" He jogged alongside as Todd strode away from the arbor.

Todd groaned. It was bad enough he had to listen to Sam spewing that trash. Now he had to listen to Watts too? *Tom's going to go crazy with this one,* Todd thought. *Worse, now he'll never leave me alone!*

"This is so wild!" Elizabeth shrieked as she rounded the hairpin turn, her hair streaming out from beneath her helmet. "I feel like I'm flying! I don't even feel like me!"

Elizabeth grinned at the realization. She thought back to the beginning of the summer, when she'd been studying with Nina for finals. It was hard to connect that serious, studious girl who was so worried about her art-history class with the one who was racing in Daytona Beach, Florida.

"Go, Elizabeth!" Charlie yelled from the sidelines as Elizabeth passed the yellow-and-black-checkered flag.

Expertly Elizabeth brought the car to a halt. "What's my time?" She took off her helmet and looked up at the racetrack attendant.

"You may not be ready for the 500 yet, but you're off to a good start." He grinned as he walked over to the car with a stopwatch in his hand. "You knocked three seconds off your last round."

Elizabeth flung her helmet in the air with a whoop and caught it neatly. "Not bad, huh?" *And you're not bad either,* she thought as she took in the attendant's sparkling blue eyes and great build. She flashed him a breathtaking smile. The guy looked her up and down and smiled back. Elizabeth was gratified by his reaction. *Hey, I haven't lived with Jessica Wakefield for eighteen years for nothing!* she thought, and laughed.

"You were awesome!" Charlie cried as she ran down from the stands and joined the attendant at Elizabeth's side.

A moment later Ruby pulled up alongside. "Hey, Elizabeth. Still want to go to Cape Canaveral?"

Elizabeth laughed again and shook her head. "No way! This is the most fun I've had in—in my entire life! Way better than driving that red Mustang I rented to get me and Jess to San Fran!"

"You think racing against the clock is fun, wait until you try racing against me! You up for it, girl?"

"Oh, I'm up for it, all right," Elizabeth replied with a gleam in her eye.

"But then I won't know who to root for," Charlie said. "I don't want to take sides!"

"Tell you what," Elizabeth said. "Charlie, you root for both of us because it doesn't matter who wins. I'm taking all three of us out for drinks later!"

"Awesome!"

"Hey, it's the least I could do," Elizabeth said, looking at Ruby. "If it weren't for you guys, I never would have gotten behind the wheel of a race car."

It's true, she thought as she regarded Charlie and Ruby with affection. *I've learned so much from them this summer. And only a few weeks ago I was wondering how I was going to survive to the end of the trip with them!*

Elizabeth put her helmet back on. *Even if I don't win the five-thousand-dollar scholarship,* she said to herself, *I'm definitely richer for this summer. I'm going home with something even more important than money—new friendships.*

"Let's go!" she yelled to Ruby as she slammed her foot down on the gas pedal and tore off, leaving a cloud of dust in her wake.

"I still wish we'd stopped in Orlando," Rob grumbled. "And we could have parked there too, instead of having to take that expensive cab ride into town."

"Disney World is for kids." Jessica snorted. "Palm Beach is for grown-ups." She pushed her sunglasses back on her head and looked appreciatively at the glittering array of shops spread out in front of them.

"I think Disney World would have been fun," Tom said. "Then again, are we *sure* we didn't hit

Disney World after all?" He gestured toward a woman who was walking two poodles, one dyed pink and the other dyed blue. Both dogs wore giant diamond collars. "You can't tell me they're not some kind of act."

"Sorry, guys." Neil shrugged. "It was a judgment call. You were all asleep, and I figured that we wouldn't have much time to hang at Disney anyway. We have only an hour or two, and I've heard you can wait that long just to get on some of the rides."

"So, what should we do now that we're here?" Pam asked.

Neil paused. He knew what he wanted to do. He wanted to hang out with Jessica, maybe hit the stores, have lunch someplace funky. He wanted to have *fun* with Jessica.

The way we did before I told her I was gay, he thought, with a mixture of anger and sorrow. He wasn't one hundred percent sure where Jessica's hostility was coming from. He still clung to a little shred of doubt that it had anything to do with his revelation. He glanced at her, but as usual, she was avoiding his eyes.

Neil sighed. "Well, I promised my family I'd bring home some gifts. I don't know about the rest of you, but I'm going shopping."

"Me too!" Jessica announced.

Neil quirked an eyebrow at her. What's going on? he wondered. Was Jessica finally coming around? Maybe she wanted to make up. . . .

Neil nearly laughed out loud as he realized what Jessica was up to. She didn't want to make up. She just didn't want Neil to scoop her on any fabulous purchases! Jessica was bound and determined to outshop him. His purchase of the inlaid picture frame probably still rankled. Neil figured that she would buy anything he showed an interest in just to stop him from getting his hands on it.

Well, there was more than one way to play that game, he thought wickedly as he turned on his heel and headed for the most expensive shop he could find.

Chapter Seven

"I just have to have these," Neil said to the saleswoman. "They're absolutely perfect. But I need a size thirteen, extra narrow. Would you see if you have any?"

His feet don't look that big, Jessica thought as she peeked out from behind a rack of men's ties. Her eyes narrowed as she took in the merchandise that Neil was holding up for the salesclerk's inspection.

Purple rubber boots? What would anyone want with purple rubber boots! When Neil's back was turned, she dashed out from behind the tie rack and scooped up a pair in size six.

"They must be really hip in the Bay Area," she mumbled as she rummaged through her purse. Finally she came up with a fistful of wrinkled bills. She hastily handed the boots and the bills to another salesclerk hovering around the shoe department. "Hurry up," she hissed as she kept an eye on Neil.

"Sorry, sir, we don't have your size," the sales-clerk said apologetically to Neil as Jessica's clerk returned with a large shopping bag.

"Gee, that's too bad. I really liked them." The corners of Neil's mouth drooped, and Jessica thought he looked terribly unhappy.

"Ha!" Jessica crowed. She couldn't wait to get back to the Winnebago. She'd put on the purple boots and parade around in them. Neil would be so jealous, he might never recover!

Jessica scampered after Neil as he walked across the floor to the men's sweater department. For the past half hour she'd been shadowing his every move as he led her a merry and expensive chase around one of Palm Beach's most exclusive de-partment stores.

Jessica looked down at the pile of shopping bags by her side in alarm. She was growing dis-mally low on cash, and she'd maxed out one of her credit cards a long time ago, but there was no way she was going to let Neil scoop her on any-thing.

At least he hasn't outshopped me this time, Jessica thought smugly. If anything, she had outshopped him! Neil hadn't made one single purchase!

"You wouldn't think he'd be so hard to fit," she murmured as she looked at Neil's tall, broad-shouldered frame. *Oh, well, what does it matter,* she decided. *The important thing is that I'm getting all the fabulous—OK, weird—items Neil wants!*

Now that's more like it, Jessica thought when she saw Neil pawing through a pile of cashmere sweaters. He held up a particularly glorious pullover in crimson. Perfect for a chilly night. Jessica nodded in approval. But . . . She kind of hoped Neil would pass on the cashmere. She was beginning to feel a little queasy about her financial situation.

"I barely have enough for a stick of gum," she muttered as she glanced in her empty wallet.

"This is perfect!" Neil exclaimed.

Jessica looked up again to see him holding another cashmere sweater—in an awful muddy brown. "I just have to have it. Do you think it comes in an extra, extra large?"

Jessica sighed.

"Hey, watch where you're going!" The car screeched to a halt, and the driver stuck his head out of the window. "You better be more careful, sonny!" he yelled.

But Todd barely noticed. He raced across the street as if he were being pursued by the Furies. Was Tom still following him? He glanced nervously over his shoulder.

He heaved a sigh of relief when he saw that the coast was clear. Todd drew a hand across his brow and slowed his pace as he gulped in several large lungfuls of air. He was seriously lucky. He could have . . .

"Tom!"

Tom stood directly in front of him, his powerful frame completely blocking the sidewalk.

"I thought I'd lost you!" Todd cried.

"Never try and outrun a quarterback," Tom said sternly. "I almost got hit by a car back there when I followed you through the intersection. But don't worry, I forgive you. Look," he continued as he fell into step beside Todd, "we've got to focus on Sam. I didn't catch all of the conversation. When is he going to meet this other girl? Did he say what he was going to do with Elizabeth? Did he mention kissing her again?"

"No!" Todd wailed. He clapped his hands over his ears to block out Tom's incessant chatter. For the past forty-five minutes, until he'd managed to escape, Tom had been peppering him with questions, plans, and flat-out wild schemes about how they could rescue Elizabeth from Sam's clutches. Todd still cared about Elizabeth, and he was as determined as Watts to see that she didn't get hurt, but he couldn't listen to Tom for another second or he'd go crazy!

"Where did Sam say this girl lives? Do you think we should tell Elizabeth? How much does she know? Can we slip something in his drink?"

When does he stop to breathe? Todd wondered. He looked about in desperation, hoping to find another escape route or place to hide. His eyes scanned the busy thoroughfare.

The pet store? Nah. Unfair to the animals. The fast-food place? Too small. Tom would catch him in a second. What about that department store?

Todd looked up at the large, granite structure as if it were the answer to all his prayers. He knew that inside were miles of cosmetics, floors of dresses and suits, escalators and elevators . . . The perfect place to give someone the slip!

Todd plunged across the street just as the light turned green, leaving Tom behind in a stream of traffic. He ran up the marble steps that led to the entrance and flung himself through the revolving doors.

"Safe!" he cried as he sagged against the wall. He closed his eyes for a brief second as a wave of relief rolled over him.

"Todd!"

His eyes flew open at the sound of his name. *Whew.* It was only Jessica. She came toward him, staggering under the weight of a dozen shopping bags.

"Perfect! Just the person I wanted to see," she purred, dumping the bags at his feet. "I've run out of money, Todd, and I need your help. I've got to get these plaid handkerchiefs. Do you mind?"

Out of the frying pan . . . Todd shook his head in defeat, grabbed up the shopping bags, and followed Jessica to the cash register.

*   *   *

"What's his problem?" Tom muttered angrily. *You'd think I have the plague or something! I just want to figure out strategy!* He shook his head in irritation as he waited for the light to change.

I've got to work again with Wilkins on this one. Tom nodded decisively. Todd knew the score. And even though Todd had never had the kind of deep, meaningful, adult relationship Tom had had with Elizabeth, he really did have her best interests at heart.

The light changed, and Tom threaded his way through the traffic toward the department store. He sprinted up the steps and charged through the door with as much determination and energy as if he were trying to score a winning touchdown.

He should be around here somewhere. . . . Tom frowned as he scanned the floor in search of Todd. Racks and racks of silk scarves and handbags, miles of cosmetics and perfumes . . . but no Todd.

Suddenly Tom spotted a head of black hair several yards away. Neil. And there was Jessica, skulking a few steps behind. And there was Todd, slightly behind Jessica! What were they doing— playing follow the leader?

Tom couldn't help but laugh as he drew closer and watched Neil walk through the men's accessory department, picking up and discarding items nonchalantly. Jessica pounced on every item Neil had considered and threw it to a very happy salesclerk to ring up. Todd followed, handing his credit card to the salesclerk and adding the shopping bag to the ever growing pile he was carrying.

"Todd!" Tom called, jogging over to join his friend. "You don't have time to shop. We have to figure out what to do about Sam. We don't have much time before the last event!"

"Boy, am I glad to see you!" Todd said as Jessica tossed a silver lamé scarf on Todd's head. "You are so the person I need."

"You are? I am?" Tom asked in surprise. See? He knew Wilkins wasn't such a bad guy after all. Todd knew he needed Tom's help if he wanted to protect Elizabeth from Burgess!

"Yeah." Todd dumped the shopping bags at Tom's feet. He plucked the silver lamé scarf from his head and carefully arranged it around Tom's shoulders. "You can carry these," he said with a twinkle in his eye.

"Tom! Hurry up!" Jessica cried, skidding to a stop before Tom and Todd. "Neil's getting away! Honestly, some people are so slow!" she added impatiently as she flung a large straw hat with a trailing ribbon on Tom's head.

"Huh?" Tom gaped at her, then looked back toward the exit, where Todd was making his getaway.

"Tom!" Jessica shrilled, grabbing him by the sleeve. "I said, hurry up!"

Tom was totally lost. There was no way he'd be able to catch up with Todd. With a deep, heartfelt sigh he trudged after Jessica.

"Tom!" Jessica's voice was tinged with irritation. "You forgot to pay!"

"Oh, I'm paying all right," Tom said through gritted teeth. "I'm paying big time!"

"This is most nice." Uli smiled as he slicked sunblock over his arms. "It's much better than a racetrack, no?"

"You're not kidding," Josh said with a grin. He lowered the pair of binoculars he was using to scan the beach for babes. "I'm glad we took a break from the girls. Who wants to go to a racetrack when you can enjoy this kind of scenery instead?" His eyes followed two spectacularly well-endowed blondes in string bikinis as they sauntered down the beach.

"There is not much scenery." Uli frowned. "Just the water. And maybe the sand."

"Not that kind of scenery, Uli." Sam yawned as he turned over to toast his back. "Josh means the local talent."

"The talent?" Uli repeated, baffled. "But there are no musical acts. What do you mean?"

Sam sighed. As much as he liked Uli, it was tiresome having to explain so many things to him all the time. "He means the babes," he said.

Uli's brow cleared. "Oh. Why didn't you say so? But they are not so much. In Sweden the girls, they are all going topless."

"Did you hear that?" Josh elbowed Sam. "Topless!

I don't know about you, guy, but as soon as I get back to school, I'm applying for a transfer to Stockholm."

Sam grimaced as he touched his ribs where Josh had nudged him. *Maybe it's not Uli I'm getting tired of. Maybe it's Josh.*

"Robobabe closing in at three o'clock," Josh yelped. "You've got to check this one out, Sam. C'mon, you want to have something to tell your grandchildren, don't you?"

Sam rolled over onto his back. He was royally bored. Josh's particular brand of adolescent charm was growing thinner by the second. Sam stared at Josh as Josh stared at the girl. Josh's tongue was hanging out of his mouth, and his eyes were bugging out of his head. He looked like an insect.

"Did you see that?" Josh demanded when the girl had passed by. "Did you?"

"Sorry. I wasn't looking," Sam said wearily. "Look, I'm really tired. I'm going to try and catch some sleep."

"Hey," Josh protested. "The time for sleep is when you're six feet under. Sometimes I wonder about you, dude."

"Great. You do that." Sam closed his eyes and prepared to ignore Josh.

"I mean, there's an entire feast—tons of eye candy!—laid out in front of you, right here on this beach, and you don't even pay any attention. You know what your problem is?"

"Tell me," Sam said dryly.

"You've let Elizabeth get to you." Josh regarded Sam seriously. "I mean, sure, you're hooking up with Angelina in Miami. But right now you can't enjoy yourself because you're totally under Elizabeth's spell. It's like she's controlling your actions when she's not even here. I just don't get what you see in her." Josh sneered. "It's not like she's all over you or anything. I mean, that I could get."

Sam opened one eye and squinted up at Josh. Was Josh right? he wondered. *Am I totally under Elizabeth's spell? Is she controlling me?* It was not a pleasant thought. Sam was used to living life on his terms and according to his own rules.

"Nobody controls Sam Burgess," he muttered angrily. He grabbed the binoculars out of Josh's hands and raised them to his eyes.

"Robobabe at three hundred yards," he said with a smirk as he eyed a particularly delicious brunette.

"Hey, dude." Josh slapped him on the back. "I'm glad to see you're back in the game."

So am I, Sam thought. *So am I.*

Chapter Eight

"I can't believe we're not going to be sleeping here tonight," Charlie said as she stripped her bed and folded the sheets.

The girls were cleaning out the Winnebago—prior to leaving it forever. They'd arrived in Miami, and the next stop on their itinerary was the tarmac where the prop planes would be waiting to take them to Key West.

Sam, Uli, and Josh had already packed their bags and left. *Of course, they didn't even bother to help us clean,* Charlie thought angrily. She picked up a sponge and began wiping down the table.

"I can't believe we're going to sleep in real beds tonight," Ruby said as she packed up her sheet music and stuffed some T-shirts in her duffel bag.

"And I, for one, can't wait!" Elizabeth poked her head out of the storage cupboard she was cleaning. "Just think. Freshly laundered sheets, lots of hot water, fluffy towels . . ." Her voice trailed off dreamily.

"You're forgetting room service," Ruby pointed out. "No more of this fast-food junk. I can't believe my complexion has made it this far without a major rebellion. Hey, Charlie, what have you missed most about civilization these past four weeks?"

"Scott," Charlie murmured with a small smile on her face. She blushed as both Elizabeth and Ruby burst out laughing. She was glad they were both getting along so well, and she was enjoying their company more than she'd ever thought she would. But that didn't mean she wasn't still feeling confused and lonely. She just wasn't comfortable talking too much about her pregnancy with her new friends. She wanted to talk about it with her boyfriend. Face-to-face.

I really need to talk to Scott! Charlie's eyes misted over as she thought about the last time they'd had a real, in-person conversation. Oh, sure, they spoke on the phone almost every day, but only for a few minutes at a time. Charlie thought he'd have caught up with Team Two again by now. . . .

"Are you OK?" Elizabeth asked quietly. Charlie looked up to find Elizabeth staring at her intently.

"I'm fine," Charlie said unconvincingly as she tied the strings on her duffel bag.

"You sure?" Ruby chimed in. "You look a little green. Is it . . . You know."

"Morning sickness?" Charlie laughed and gestured at the late afternoon sun that streamed through the large front window. "No. Actually, morning sickness can last all day, but I haven't felt nauseous in a while. What I really feel is homesick."

"Homesick?" Elizabeth asked. "You mean, you miss OCC?"

"I think I know just what our little Charlie needs," Ruby said, looking out the window. "And I have a feeling she's going to get it too. Real soon."

"Hmmm," Elizabeth said, trying to hide a grin. "I see what you mean."

"What are you guys up to?" Charlie frowned. "You look like you've got some big secret or something."

Elizabeth and Ruby shared a quick look and then, grabbing their duffel bags, they scurried out of the Winnebago.

"What are you doing!" Charlie called out after them. "Where did they . . . Scott!" Charlie gasped. Scott stood in the doorway of the Winnebago, a warm smile on his face.

"I made it," he whispered as Charlie flung himself in his arms. "I'm flying to Miami with you. Do you think there'll be room on the plane?"

"There'd better be," Charlie said laughingly as

she smothered him with kisses. "Because I'm not letting you out of my sight ever again!"

"It looks a little small," Elizabeth said as she stood on the tarmac along with the members of all the other teams and looked at the prop plane. "Are we sure this thing really flies?"

"What's the matter? You're not scared, are you?" Josh asked. Josh pushed by Elizabeth and boarded the tiny aircraft.

"I've flown in plenty of propeller planes before," Alison Quinn said, smirking at Elizabeth. "There's nothing to be nervous about. They can get a little bumpy, of course, but it's nothing compared to something like white-water rafting. Oh, sorry! I forgot." She raised a haughty eyebrow. "Your team fell apart on that event, didn't it, Elizabeth? Well, then, I guess you would be nervous."

Leave it to Alison, Elizabeth thought as she watched her flounce off to the plane.

"Leave it to Alison," a voice whispered in her ear.

"Jessica!" Elizabeth exclaimed, throwing her arms around her sister. "Let's sit together on the plane, OK?"

"I think we're supposed to sit with our teams," Danny Wyatt said as he came up behind them. "Hey, Elizabeth, you looked pretty good on the battlefield the other day. Too bad your team came in second."

146

"Gee, thanks," Elizabeth said dryly. "I sure hope we win this event."

"Anybody know what it is?" Alisha Korn asked, hefting her duffel bag on her shoulder. "I hope it's something easy. I'm pretty wiped." Suddenly she grinned. "Hey, I've never seen you guys standing side by side before. You really *are* identical!"

Elizabeth laughed. "That's what our birth certificates say. But it's easy to tell us apart. Just look at the way we dress." Jessica's face was made up with powder, lipstick, and mascara, and her hair was loose. She wore a purple halter and white short-shorts, and on her feet, white platform sneakers.

Elizabeth, on the other hand, was makeup free and wore her hair in a no-nonsense ponytail. Her baby-blue-and-white button-down shirt was tucked into a pair of classic chinos, and on her feet she sported baby blue skips.

Alison raised her eyebrows. "Oh yeah. On second thought, you guys look *real* different. C'mon, I'm boarding this thing."

Elizabeth looked at her sister. "Let's go, Jess."

"Right with you, Liz."

Elizabeth and Jessica boarded. Elizabeth stowed her duffel bag in the overhead compartment and glanced around the plane's cramped interior. Charlie looked so happy sitting next to Scott. But that meant . . . Elizabeth frowned as she realized the only free seat was next to Sam

147

since Uli was sitting with one of the ICSN cameramen. *I don't believe it,* she thought angrily.

Elizabeth could see by the expression on Jessica's face that her sister was no happier about her own seating arrangements. Elizabeth wondered why Jessica would be against sitting with Neil. *Sometimes there's no figuring Jess,* she thought as she climbed over several people to settle down next to Sam.

"You don't look too happy," he commented as she fastened her seat belt. "What's the matter? You don't want to sit with me? Well, it's Charlie's fault," he grumbled. "If that boyfriend of hers hadn't tagged along, the seating arrangements wouldn't be screwed up."

"Leave Charlie out of this," Elizabeth replied stiffly. She took a paperback out of her purse and flipped it open.

Sam shrugged. "Whatever you say." He turned away and began to fiddle with the buttons on his armrests as the plane taxied down the runway.

The takeoff was anything but smooth. Elizabeth closed her book as her stomach began doing push-ups against her ribs.

C'mon, girl, she told herself sternly. *You've flown a million times before. There's nothing to be afraid of!*

But Elizabeth still felt a little queasy as the plane bounced around. "It feels like the clouds are playing football with the plane," she murmured.

Her hand clamped down on the armrest—and Sam's hand—unconsciously.

"Oh!" Elizabeth gasped as the plane took a sudden nosedive. Pam Cox and Cynthia Lewis screamed. Alison Quinn had turned a sickly shade of green.

"We're going to crash!" someone yelled.

Elizabeth gripped Sam's hand convulsively. She took several deep breaths to try and calm herself, but it didn't help. She'd never been on such a bumpy flight in her life. It was almost impossible not to feel frightened!

"C'mon, that's not good," Sam said, leaning close to her, his breath tickling her cheek. "You're only going to hyperventilate taking deep breaths. Breathe more normally," he instructed as he covered her hand with his. He spoke gently, as if Elizabeth were a little girl, and she felt some of the terror that gripped her begin to dissolve. "In, out. C'mon, that's right. In, out."

Elizabeth followed his lead, and her heart rate slowed slightly. "Thank you," she managed to gasp. Once again she was touched and amazed at Sam's concern. Once again the nasty, sarcastic mask had fallen away, revealing the deep, sensitive guy who lived underneath. At that moment, staring deeply into Sam's eyes, Elizabeth forgot their past troubles. "I don't think I like prop planes," she said weakly.

"There's not really a lot of turbulence in the

atmosphere," Sam said soothingly as he stroked her hand. "It's just that small planes like this get buffeted about more easily."

"Not a lot of turbulence?" Elizabeth's voice shook as the plane bounced unmercifully. "You could have fooled me!"

"Try to think of something else," Sam urged, increasing the pressure on her hand and leaning even closer. As if he were about to wrap her in his arms. Elizabeth still felt sick to her stomach, but she was comforted by his closeness. Again she tried to remember why she was angry at him, but couldn't.

"Pretend you aren't on this plane right now," Sam whispered. "What would you rather be doing more than anything?"

"What would I rather be doing more than anything?" Elizabeth considered the question thoughtfully as she returned Sam's soulful gaze. "Uh, I guess I'd rather be, uh . . ."

Elizabeth's voice trailed off as the answer to Sam's question hit her. *Right now, more than anything, I'd rather be kissing you, Sam Burgess. And if the plane crashed and we went down, I wouldn't even mind as long as I got to kiss you one more time.*

"Are you scared?" Neil asked. Jessica could see that his hands were gripping the armrest so hard, his knuckles were turning white.

Scared? I left scared back on the runway,

Jessica thought. *I'm flat-out terrified!* Still, there was no way she was going to admit the truth to Neil.

"S-S-Scared? M-M-Me? Forget a-about it!" Jessica said with chattering teeth. "I'm not afraid of anything. Oooh!" The plane dipped sharply into the clouds. Jessica felt her stomach slide toward her throat and let go of the armrest to clap a hand over her mouth. Suddenly the plane shot upward and she was thrown against her seat.

"Well, that's good because I'm not scared either," Neil said tightly. "I think this is fun." Neil flashed a sickly grin. "It's like a really stellar ride at a fabulous amusement park."

Jessica unpeeled herself from the back of her seat. "Sure. It's great," she said. "Just like Disney World. In fact, I'm having such a good time, I don't want the flight to ever end!" Jessica could almost feel her face turning three shades of puce, but she managed to return Neil's smile.

"Yeah." Neil swallowed convulsively. "I could do this forever."

Jessica couldn't answer. The plane hit a particularly bad pocket of turbulence, and she closed her eyes to mutter a silent prayer.

"Jessica?" Neil said quietly.

"Yes?" Jessica whispered. She didn't dare look at him. She knew that if she did, Neil would see the terror lurking in her eyes.

"It's OK," Neil said. He managed to pry his

hand loose from the armrest and place it over hers. "I'm scared too."

"You are?" Jessica grasped his hand as if it were a lifeline.

"Uh-huh. In fact, I hate flying to begin with. This is worse than my wildest nightmare." He paused and lowered his voice. "I'm so afraid we're going to crash."

The plane lurched, and Jessica was thrown sideways against him. "Well, look at the bright side," she said, forcing herself upright. "If we do crash, it won't matter anymore that we're in last place."

"That's true," Neil said thoughtfully. "And you know what else? We'll never have to play truth or dare again."

"You know what's even better?" Jessica said with a small grin. "We'll never again have to hear Pam call Rob 'snookums.'"

Neil laughed. "Jessica, you're the only person in the world who could make me laugh on the brink of death!"

"What would you *rather be doing more than anything?"* Elizabeth's words rang in his head as Sam staggered off the plane and toward the group of rental cars that stood waiting on the tarmac.

His legs were shaking so badly, he could barely walk. He knew that Josh was talking to him, but he was in too much shock to understand what his teammate was saying. He waved away the keys Josh was dangling in front of his face and slid into the passenger seat of the sports utility vehicle ICSN had provided. Sam didn't feel up to driving. The world seemed to be spinning around him, and he had serious doubts that it would ever stop.

It wasn't the flight that had rattled him so badly. He liked flying, and a little rockiness never bothered him. He'd been happy to console Elizabeth. He'd wanted to take her mind off the flight, so he'd asked her a simple question, the kind of question that doesn't really mean anything. Like, What would you do if you won a million dollars in the lottery?

Elizabeth hadn't answered the question, but she'd calmed down and things had been fine. Until she asked him the same question he'd asked her.

What would you rather be doing more than anything?

Sam exhaled gustily and leaned his head against the plush upholstery of the seat. His hands were still trembling as he recalled his answer. Not that he'd told Elizabeth the truth because as far as he was concerned, the truth was way too scary to admit.

What Sam really wanted to do, more than call Angelina, more than win the contest, was to kiss Elizabeth one more time. At least one more time.

What's happened to me? Sam asked himself.

How did I let Elizabeth get to me like this?

"Hey, Sam, where are you, Mars? I've been asking you to open the glove compartment for, like, the last ten minutes," Josh said impatiently.

"Huh?" Sam shook his head.

"Yeah, dude, the glove compartment. The event instructions are in there."

"Why are you in such a rush, Josh?" Ruby asked from the backseat. "I'm ready to relax, not compete. Besides, I bet the last event is a no-brainer. There probably won't even be a training session."

"That's right." Elizabeth nodded. "Anyway, what could they give us that would be so difficult down here in Key West? Snorkeling?"

"We could all stop guessing if Sam would just read the instructions already!" Josh cried.

"Sorry," Sam mumbled. He flipped open the glove compartment, reached in, and took out the ICSN envelope. He was surprised at the weight of it. It was fairly thick, like it contained something a little more substantial than fishing instructions.

"Well, go on," Josh urged. "Read them."

Sam tore open the envelope.

"The suspense is killing me," Ruby said. She yawned and flipped her hair over her shoulder. "Are we supposed to be catching marlin or salmon?"

"There is salmon in Key West?" Uli's blue eyes twinkled at the prospect.

Sam ignored the chatter and concentrated on

reading the instruction papers. *Maybe I've gone crazy,* he thought as he scanned them for a second time. He couldn't believe what he was reading.

Sam looked up from the instructions. The atmosphere in the car had suddenly become very still, as if everyone knew that something was wrong.

"Uh . . . ," Sam began uncertainly. "Has everybody made out their wills?"

"No way am I doing it!" Jessica shrieked. "They must be insane!"

"Look, Jessica," Todd said soothingly. "I know it seems kind of scary, but I'm sure things will look different in the morning. Tonight you'll have a bubble bath, maybe order some room service. . . ."

Girls liked that stuff, didn't they? Todd frowned as he navigated the car in and out of the traffic that clogged the streets of New Town.

"I don't care if I get to take a thousand bubble baths," Jessica wailed. "I don't care if I get to order room service every night for the rest of my life. I don't care if we do so well in the event tomorrow that we magically pull up to first place and win. There's *no way* I'm going to jump off a cliff, and that's final!"

"Uh, it does seem a little extreme." Todd thought Tom looked about as shell-shocked as Jessica. "I mean, white-water rafting was bad enough. But riding a bike off a cliff?"

"I've never heard anything like it," Rob said, his mouth set in a grim line, his hand clutching Pam's. Todd glanced in the rearview mirror. It was clear from the expression on Pam's face that she shared Jessica's fears.

"The instructions don't say we have to ride our bikes off the cliff," Neil explained as he pored over the papers. "They just say we have to ride our bikes up a really steep cliff that juts out over the ocean. We ditch the bikes at the edge, and then we jump off the cliff."

"Yeah, just like Tom said. We ride our bikes over a cliff!" Jessica grabbed the handle of the door and shook it wildly.

"What are you doing?" Todd yelped.

"Trying to escape," she shot back.

"Neil, will you stop her, please?" Todd sighed. "Look, Jessica, this news is stressful enough without you causing a traffic accident."

"What's the training session supposed to be?" Pam croaked. "Are we supposed to learn CPR or how to set broken bones or something?"

"Probably." Jessica nodded. "This thing is just too crazy."

"Look," Todd said patiently as he turned right onto Flamingo Street, "this whole ICSN competition is a big publicity opportunity for the sponsors, right?"

"Right." Jessica shrugged. "So what?"

"So, the sponsors aren't going to risk bad

publicity. Do you think they'd allow us to participate in an event that was seriously dangerous? C'mon, Jess, I'm sure this last event is easy as pie. Didn't you see the movie *Six Days, Seven Nights?* Remember how the hero and heroine jumped off a cliff? They were just fine," Todd concluded with a reassuring smile.

"Todd," Jessica snapped impatiently. "That was a movie. Not real life. Those actors had stunt doubles. Or else the scene was done with computer imaging."

"Still, Todd has a point," Neil said calmly. "There's no way the sponsors would risk the bad publicity that would follow if one of the contestants got hurt. And believe me, Jessica, there'd be *plenty* of bad publicity for the sponsors and ICSN if one of us got hurt."

"Yeah, think about it," Tom chimed in. "There's got to be some catch. This stunt is probably a lot easier than it sounds on paper."

Jessica chewed on her lower lip and after a moment relaxed her grip on the door handle. Todd flashed Tom and Neil a grateful look. *Thanks, guys,* he said silently.

Pam grabbed the instructions from Neil. "It says here the cliff is one of the highest in the Keys," she said shrilly. "It says here there's a fifty-foot drop to the water!"

Todd glared at her in the rearview mirror.

Jessica grabbed the door handle again and

pushed open the door. Neil grabbed the hem of her T-shirt, pulled her back inside, and shut the door after her.

"What are you doing?" Todd yelled.

"Same thing as before," Jessica yelled back. "Trying to escape!"

Todd sighed as he pulled into the parking lot of their hotel. "Jessica," he said gently, "I know you don't want to do this event, but I, for one, haven't come all this way just to be disqualified. Again! It's the last event. Will you just do it—for the team?"

"The team's in last place," Jessica said stubbornly. "There's no way we can win. I say we bail."

"We could still pull up," Neil interjected. "At least get out of last place. Anyway, now that I think about it, the event does sound kind of exciting."

"At least stick around for the training event, Jess," Todd said reasonably. "Maybe it won't be as bad as you think."

"Maybe," Jessica muttered.

Tom stepped out of the car. "I say we forget about the event until tomorrow," he suggested. "Why don't we just have some fun? Key West looks like a pretty neat place."

"Yeah," Neil said as he joined Tom on the pavement. "Let's have a really good dinner."

"Sounds great," Todd said. "Right, Jess?"

No answer.

Todd shook his head as he walked toward the hotel lobby. *Oh yeah. It'll be real easy to have fun,* he thought. All he had to do was figure out how to keep Sam away from Elizabeth, prevent Jessica from bailing—and work up the nerve to jump off a cliff!

"Duval Street is supposed to have really great restaurants," Ruby said as she consulted her guidebook.

"You mean *expensive* restaurants," Josh grumbled as Team Two walked out of their hotel in Old Town in search of dinner.

"It's so beautiful here," Elizabeth said as she looked around at the old clapboard houses highlighted by the glow of the setting sun. "I can see why Ernest Hemingway and Tennessee Williams loved it so much. Everybody seems so laid-back. And the weather's so balmy."

"That's because Key West is the southernmost point in the States," Scott explained, draping an arm around Charlie and pulling her close. "It's the end of the line."

Is it the end of the line for Sam and me too? Elizabeth wondered. She glanced at Sam, walking a few paces ahead with Josh and Uli. Elizabeth had an uncomfortable feeling that Sam was avoiding her. He'd barely said two words to her since they'd deplaned. *But we were so close on the plane,*

159

she thought. She had thought all the barriers were down at last. But hadn't she thought that before—and been wrong?

"Hey, Elizabeth," Ruby said, looking up from her guidebook. "You want to have a drink at Hemingway's favorite bar? It's only a few blocks from here."

Elizabeth shook her head. "No, thanks. But I am going on a tour of his house after the training session tomorrow."

"If I were you, I'd go now," Josh muttered darkly. "Who knows if any of us will be alive after the training session."

Elizabeth shivered in spite of the warm air. There was no denying this last event sounded pretty scary. She was nervous about it, and from the way the conversation had just died, she knew she wasn't the only one.

"Maybe we should head over to Mallory Dock instead of Duval Street," Elizabeth said cheerfully, trying to dissolve the gloom that had descended on her teammates. "It's supposed to be pretty wild, and I'm sure there are fun places to eat. C'mon," she urged. "It's only a block and a half in the other direction."

Josh shrugged. "We might as well have fun before we croak."

A few minutes later they turned into Mallory Dock. Elizabeth was blown away. She'd heard the dock was a wild place, but nothing could have prepared her for the snake charmers, fire-eaters, and jugglers that filled the small square.

"I should have brought my guitar!" Ruby wailed.

"This looks like a good place for dinner," Charlie said, stopping before one of the small cafés clustered around the square. "Who's up for conch fritters and key lime pie?"

"It sounds most American," Uli said as he sat down on one of the chairs at the table Charlie had chosen.

"It sounds yummy," Elizabeth said, smiling at the way Scott pulled out a wicker chair for Charlie. Since Scott had joined them in Miami, Elizabeth had been both relieved and impressed by the way he treated Charlie. It was obvious they really loved each other and that whatever problems they faced, they faced together.

Elizabeth was happy for Charlie and Scott. Still, she couldn't help but feel a little wistful at the sight of two people so much in love. *Scott's so incredibly tender toward Charlie,* Elizabeth thought with a small sigh. Her eyes darted over to where Sam was sprawled at one of the neighboring tables. He appeared to be totally oblivious to her existence.

It wasn't that she wanted him hovering around as if she were some fragile piece of glass, Elizabeth thought as she watched Scott arrange a lacy shawl around Charlie's shoulders. She flipped open her menu with a frown and eyed Sam over the top of it. Josh was whispering something in his ear, and from the expression on Sam's face, it was something stupid.

She didn't need—or want—Sam to hover around her every second. Suddenly Sam's eyes met hers, and he quickly looked away. Elizabeth frowned in irritation. But she did wish he could bring himself to look her in the eye!

Sam sighed unhappily and pushed away his plate. The conch fritters had tasted like burned rubber, and he hated key lime pie. But the bad meal wasn't why he was in such a bad mood. He simply couldn't shake the feeling of uneasiness that had gripped him ever since he'd realized—on the plane—how much Elizabeth meant to him.

You're just attracted to her, he told himself for the hundredth time since that afternoon. *It's just a summer fling. Hey, it's not even a summer fling,* he reassured himself. *We've only kissed a couple of times.*

Sam leaned back in his chair and watched as Ruby softly sang the words to a new love song she'd written. Uli, Charlie, Scott, and Elizabeth seemed to be enjoying it. But Sam couldn't help rolling his eyes over the sappy words.

"I know what you mean," Josh said as he wiped a dot of whipped cream off his chin. "All that stuff about true love gives me the heebie-jeebies." He threw his napkin down on the table and pushed back his chair.

"You're telling me," Sam responded heartily. Josh was right. Love was just a crock, the kind of thing that girls like Ruby wrote stupid songs about. Love hadn't kept his mother at home with his father and her son. What did it mean anyway— love?

Sam glanced over at Elizabeth, who was now completely engrossed in conversation with Charlie and Scott. Her face was animated, and she looked especially pretty in the glow of the candlelight.

So what? Sam asked himself. *So she's pretty. Lots of girls are. Who cares?*

"Hey, let's not dwell on scary subjects," Josh said, taking a sip of beer. "Let's focus on the positive. See those girls over there?" He waved the bottle in the direction of a group of girls who were sitting at another café across the square.

Sam had to admit the girls were good-looking—if you liked the flashy, big-haired type. Sam scratched his chin thoughtfully as he looked at them. Before this summer he'd always thought he *was* attracted to the flashy, big-haired type. But as he regarded the girls across the square, he was forced to admit his tastes had changed.

"Think we should go over and talk to them?" Josh quirked an eyebrow at Sam.

"No," Sam said emphatically. "I don't think so."

Josh frowned at him. "What's your problem? They're hot."

I wish I knew. Sam shook his head ruefully as he poked the remains of the conch fritters with his fork. *Why am I stopping myself? I should just waltz right over there and buy that blonde a drink.*

"Oh, that's right. I keep forgetting." Josh grinned. "You don't have to make an effort. You've got your sure thing lined up. So, when are you going to call her?"

"It's probably too late now," Sam said uncomfortably. He had planned to call Angelina as soon as he hit Key West. But every time he caught himself thinking of how delectable she looked in that bikini, Elizabeth's face flashed before his eyes. He was disgusted by his indecisiveness.

"Too late?" Josh looked at Sam in amazement. "It's barely nine-thirty."

"Oh yeah." Sam made a show of checking his watch. "I thought it was later."

"You better call her, guy," Josh said seriously. "I can see what's happening. You're letting the Wakefield chick get to you. Don't go down that route, buddy," he warned. "Take it from me— that's a mighty dangerous road."

"You're right," Sam said slowly. "It is dangerous." He looked back at Elizabeth, and his heart gave a little lurch.

Maybe the rest of the team was frightened of jumping off the cliff, but Sam could handle that.

Jumping off a cliff was a no-brainer compared to what he was facing.

Sam looked away from Elizabeth, his mouth set in a grim line. He was in Key West to compete, not to get involved with a girl. He'd jump off the cliff. Maybe he'd break his neck. Maybe he'd even get eaten by a shark. That was OK. The one thing he was *not* going to do was fall in love.

Chapter Nine

The sun was dazzlingly bright, and the sea air was crisp. Todd took a deep breath as he adjusted his sunglasses and looked around. The ICSN crew was out in full force, busily setting up a buffet table and distributing the mountain bikes the teams were going to use for the training session.

In contrast to the frenetic activity of the crew, the members of the four teams stood clustered at the bottom of the cliff, speaking quietly to one another. Not even the fresh coffee, doughnuts, and muffins seemed to perk them up.

I guess Jessica isn't the only one frightened out of her wits, Todd thought as he surveyed the other teams. Alison Quinn looked as if she was about to faint, and Danny Wyatt looked decidedly less cheerful than usual.

"It looks like a beautiful morning to die," Tom said glumly.

"I don't know why the ICSN people are so chipper this morning," Rob muttered as he accepted a bike from one of the crew.

"Why shouldn't they be?" Jessica let her bike fall to the ground. "They're not the ones who are going to be flinging themselves off a cliff."

"We're not going off the cliff today," Todd said calmly as he picked up Jessica's bike. "We're just riding the bikes to the top to get a look."

"Yeah, but what about tomorrow?" Pam whined.

Todd didn't know how to answer her. He had to admit that he wasn't very happy about the prospect of diving off a fifty-foot cliff either. But unlike the others, he had a few other crises to deal with. Like keeping Sam away from Elizabeth and Jessica from bailing.

Todd searched the crowd for a glimpse of Elizabeth. He spotted her blond ponytail, and he breathed a sigh of relief when he saw that Sam was alone with Josh. "Probably planning another conquest," Todd muttered.

"Listen up, everyone!" It was Richie Valentine, speaking to the crowd from his perch on the engine hood of one of the ICSN vans. Todd wasn't sure who he hated more—Richie Valentine or Ned Jackson. "Today is just the dry run . . . ha ha! You're going to ride your bikes all the way up to the top of the cliff—and I don't mind telling you that it's a pretty steep climb.

Then you can look over the edge of the cliff and see what you'll be jumping into tomorrow—that is, if you have the stomach for this insane last event!"

"Jessica!" Todd reached out and snagged her as she tried to bolt.

"How are we supposed to win this thing anyway?" Tom frowned. "The team that gets all its members in the water first wins?"

"I guess." Todd shrugged, keeping a firm hand on the collar of Jessica's shirt.

"That doesn't seem right," Neil said thoughtfully. "How will the ICSN people keep track of who actually hits the water when?"

"It'll all be on camera," Rob said. "The ICSN crew will shoot the event and rerun the tape to figure out who goes in the water when."

"Let's get going, kids," Richie Valentine called. "You can leave your bikes at the top of the cliff and walk back down if you want. The ICSN crew will pick them up—and we'll see you all bright and early tomorrow morning."

"Let's go, everyone." Todd climbed onto his bike, determined to shadow Sam and keep him from being alone with Elizabeth. He pushed off.

"Todd, don't leave me!" Jessica cried.

"Jessica, we're just riding up a hill!" Todd stopped pedaling and sighed. Sam and Josh were zooming ahead.

"Hey, it's all right." Tom rode up from behind Todd and spoke quietly. "You keep an eye on Jessica, and I'll ride after Burgess."

"Great," Todd said. Tom might be a royal pain, but at least they shared the same goal—keeping Elizabeth out of Sam's slimy clutches.

Tom sprinted ahead.

"What was that all about?" Jessica asked as she rode up alongside Todd. "You guys aren't still hung up on Elizabeth, are you?" she demanded.

"Of course not," Todd said. It was true. He *wasn't* still hung up on Elizabeth, but that didn't mean he would stand around and watch her get hurt either.

Elizabeth swallowed hard as she looked down into the swirling blue water. Waves crashed against the bottom of the cliff with a mighty roar. Her stomach churned as she tried to imagine what it would be like to jump into the pounding surf.

"I'd rather go for another ride on the prop plane," she murmured to herself as seagulls wheeled overhead. At least Sam had been holding her hand then.

Elizabeth frowned as she looked around the cliff top. There were several people from different teams, but no Sam. She glanced at the pile of discarded bikes a few feet away and wondered if he'd already gone down.

Elizabeth was disappointed. She and Sam hadn't spoken at all since the plane ride, and she was confused. The night before, at Mallory Dock, Sam had sat at another table with Josh and hadn't once come over to talk. She'd figured he was too wrapped up in watching the fire-eaters and other street performers to seek her out for an intimate conversation. But he'd barely said two words to her this morning either. Elizabeth wondered if something was wrong.

She knew she felt differently about him after the plane ride. *But maybe Sam doesn't know that,* Elizabeth realized as she turned and began to walk down the hill.

Sam! He was striding purposefully ahead of her. "Hey, Sam, wait up!" she called, hurrying after him.

Sam stopped and turned toward her. Elizabeth flashed him a radiant smile.

"Hey, watch yourself!" Sam grabbed her around the waist as she came to a breathless stop on the steep incline.

Elizabeth laughed. "How did you like the view?" she asked. Her skin tingled from the touch of his hands at her waist, and she felt a pang when he dropped them suddenly. "Pretty scary, huh?" she said as she fell into step beside him.

"Yeah," Sam said shortly.

"I never figured ICSN would throw something

like this at us," Elizabeth said. She studied his profile as they walked. His brows were knit together
in a deep frown. *What's going on with him?* she
wondered. But Sam wasn't offering any answers to
her silent questions as he trudged down the hill.

"The idea of jumping off a cliff is actually
scarier than that plane ride," Elizabeth said, hoping to remind him of their closeness the previous
day.

Sam shrugged.

Elizabeth wasn't deterred. "Of course, the
plane ride had some compensations . . . ," she
hinted broadly, skipping a few paces in front of
Sam so that she could look him in the face.

"Compensations?" he repeated.

Elizabeth rolled her eyes. "Yeah, like the great
in-flight meal service."

Sam looked at her blankly. "There wasn't any
meal service on the flight."

Elizabeth smiled sweetly at Sam. "Speaking of
meals, I heard about a great place on Duval
Street."

C'mon, she urged silently. *That's supposed to be
your cue to suggest we have dinner there—alone.*

"Yeah, so?"

Elizabeth's shoulders sagged in disappointment. Didn't he feel about her the way she felt
about him? She could have sworn that when his
eyes had gazed into hers during the awful plane
ride, they were filled with deep emotion. *Maybe*

he just doesn't get what I'm hinting at, she thought hopefully. *You know how guys don't get subtlety. Maybe I just have to ask him straight-out.*

Elizabeth took a deep breath and screwed up her courage. All of a sudden the idea of asking Sam to have dinner with her seemed the scariest thing she'd ever done.

"Sam," Elizabeth said. "Will you have dinner with me tonight?"

Sam raised his eyes to hers, and Elizabeth felt a little jolt of electricity flash pass between them. His mouth curved upward in a small smile. Elizabeth held her breath.

He's going to say yes! she thought in a burst of happiness. *We'll have a really romantic dinner, and then afterward . . .*

"Sorry," Sam said. "I have other plans."

Neil stared after Jessica as she raced across the busy intersection. He'd wanted to talk to her ever since the plane ride. But right after the training session Jessica had run down the mountain and taken off into town. Neil had followed her.

Why is she avoiding me? he asked himself as he struck out across the street in hot pursuit. *I thought we'd finally patched things up.*

Neil was more confused than ever. He was pretty sure Jessica wasn't homophobic. *There's no way she would have clung to me like that on the plane if she had a problem with the gay thing,* he thought as he reached the opposite side of the street.

He watched heads turn as Jessica pranced along in front of him. It was clear that even in a T-shirt and jeans, she had a powerful effect on men of all ages.

I bet she just eats it up, Neil thought admiringly. *She must . . . That's it!*

Neil came to a dead halt on the sidewalk. People pushed their way past him. Elbows jabbed him and shopping bags banged his knees, but Neil barely noticed. He'd just figured out why Jessica was so mad at him!

Jessica just couldn't accept the fact that Neil was not interested in her. She wanted every man gasping at her feet. Gay or not. What was the first thing she'd done after Neil had rejected her? Found herself another man to worship her! *I'm probably the first guy who's ever turned her down,* Neil guessed. *And that's only because I'm gay!*

Neil threw back his head and laughed. He felt better than he had in days. Homophobia was the stuff of nightmares, but being a little conceited— that he could deal with.

"Jessica!" he yelled as he ran after her. "Wait up!"

Jessica turned. Her expression became guarded when she saw that it was Neil. "What do you want?" she asked in a sullen voice as he caught up with her. "Are you going to reject my advances again? Or how about throw my apologies back in my face? Or now maybe you'll make fun of the fact that I was so scared of the plane crashing. Maybe you were just pretending to be scared so you could laugh at me later!"

"I'm not going to do any of those things." Neil grabbed Jessica's hand and dragged her down a side street.

"Where are you taking me?" Jessica yelped.

"Be quiet for a second." Neil backed her against a wall and stared down at her. His voice was a little harsh, but his gray eyes twinkled. "I'm not going to reject you or make fun of you," he repeated.

"You're not?" Jessica said, a small frown pleating her forehead.

"Nope." Neil shook his head. "But I do have a really big news flash for you. You know something, Miss Wakefield? You're one conceited girl."

"What!" Jessica shrieked.

"You're willing to screw up a great friendship just because your ego got a little bruised. Ever since you came back to the team, you've either ignored or insulted me, forcing me to listen to Pam and Rob's disgusting baby talk and Tom and Todd's stupid posturing. And all just because I turned you down." Neil's voice grew softer. "Jessica, I thought you hated me because I'm gay. But now I know you're just mad at me because I said no. I'm the first to say no, right?"

"Of course you're the first!" Jessica exclaimed hotly.

Neil laughed, and she scowled at him. For a second.

"We *were* getting along pretty well, weren't we?" she said, looking up at him thoughtfully. "OK, maybe I am a little conceited, but I want you to admit, right this minute, that I'm the most beautiful girl you've ever rejected."

"You're definitely the most beautiful girl I've ever rejected," Neil promised.

"Well, all right, then." Jessica smiled. "But Neil, why would I hate you because you're gay? That's crazy."

Neil's face lit up in a big smile. He caught her by the wrist and led her back onto the main thoroughfare. "Never mind that now. We've got to make up for lost time. What do you want to do? Grab some lunch? Check out Hemingway's house?"

Jessica shook her head. "Nope."

"Well, then what *do* you want to do?" Neil frowned. He looked at Jessica. And then he smiled.

"Shopping!" they cried in unison.

* * *

Sam felt like a total heel. He knew perfectly well what Elizabeth had been hinting at when she'd mentioned the restaurant on Duval Street. For a moment he'd wanted to say yes. She'd looked so beautiful as she'd skipped backward down the mountain, with the wind blowing through her blond hair and her blue-green eyes sparkling. But he had said no instead. His heart gave a little tug as he recalled how her face had fallen.

"Believe me, Elizabeth, you're better off," Sam muttered to himself as he continued slowly down the mountain. "I'm not the guy for you."

He sighed as he looked toward the bottom of the hill. He could see Elizabeth talking to some other contestants, and he had to fight the urge to run to her and fling his arms around her.

"Coward," he cursed himself.

"Hey, Sam, wait up!" Sam looked over his shoulder to see Josh jogging toward him.

"Just who I need to see," he growled under his breath. He was sick of Josh. His low-class humor had stopped being funny days ago. He couldn't stand Josh's constant smarmy references to Angelina or his sly digs about Elizabeth.

"What's up?" Sam asked wearily as Josh caught up with him. "How come you're not already at the bottom?"

Josh flashed a goofy grin. "I got sidetracked. I was talking to this really gorgeous girl, and things were getting really hot when her boyfriend showed up. Man, he was built like a linebacker! I didn't feel like taking him down, though," he said cockily. "I mean, of course I would have won, but . . ."

"Yeah, right, I'm sure you would have won," Sam said, eyeing Josh's decidedly medium frame. No way Josh could take on a linebacker and come out alive.

"What did you say?" Josh challenged.

"Why do you always talk about women like that?" Sam stopped walking and poked Josh in the chest with his finger.

"Like what? What are you talking about, dude?"

"Like they're nothing more than a piece of meat," Sam said angrily.

"Like you don't?" Josh snorted. "And anyway, so what if I do?"

"It's disgusting, that's what," Sam said. "Just because you're too immature to have a real relationship with a woman doesn't mean you have to act like women are just—toys."

"Hey, I'm not the one who's been going around with a picture of some hot babe, bragging about how you're gonna score with her," Josh shouted.

"You want to know something?" Sam yelled back. "You may not be going around with her picture, but you're the one who's so hung up on her." He reached into his pocket for Angelina's picture and the scrap of paper with her phone number on it and waved them in front of Josh.

"I am not hung up on her!" Josh's face turned red. "Look, guy, I know what this is all about. You're just really chapped because Elizabeth is such a cold fish. Well, fine, but don't take it out on me."

"If you say one more word about Elizabeth . . . I am not going to be responsible for what I do to you," Sam said, his voice dangerously quiet.

Josh stepped back a few paces. "Hey, all right, man. Don't lose your cool. Look, just call your girl, OK? You'll feel a lot better after you do."

Sam looked down at the picture of Angelina. And then he tore the picture and her phone number into shreds, sprinkling them in the air like confetti.

"Are you crazy?" Josh gasped.

"No," Sam said. "Not anymore."

"What are those guys arguing about?" Tom muttered. He'd been tailing Sam ever since he'd left his bike at the top of the mountain.

If only I could get a little closer, he thought, peeking out around the tree he'd chosen to hide behind. Although he could see Sam and Josh clearly, he couldn't hear them. And he was no lip-reader.

At least Sam wasn't still with Elizabeth. Tom's expression darkened as the image of her skipping in front of Sam flashed in his mind. The joy—and then the pain—he'd seen on Elizabeth's face as she talked to Sam had affected him like a sucker punch to the gut.

Tom snuck out from behind the tree and ran toward a clump of bushes a few feet closer to Sam and Josh. But the guys had finished talking. Tom watched in surprise as Sam shoved Josh to the ground and then marched down the mountain.

What was that about? he wondered as Josh picked himself up and ran after Sam. Clearly the guys had had an argument. But about what? Those pieces of paper Sam had torn into little pieces just a moment ago? Maybe . . .

Great, Tom thought. *I've got squat to tell Wilkins.* He grumbled as he stepped out from behind the bushes and headed down to the base of the mountain, where Todd was waiting expectantly.

Tom plastered a confident smile on his face as he strode toward Todd. *I'll just act like I know what's going on,* he decided.

"So, what did you find out?" Todd said quietly, leading Tom away from the other contestants. Tom saw Elizabeth over by the ICSN buffet table with Ruby and Charlie. Sam was chatting with Mickey James, at least several yards apart. Good.

Todd stopped. "Well?" he demanded.

Tom squinted, trying to look mysterious. "Looks like something pretty major is going down," he said.

"Yeah? Is Burgess still getting together with that girl? Does Liz know he's two-timing her?"

"Hold up." Tom raised his hand to stem the tide of Todd's questions. The minute he did so, he realized the mistake he'd made. Now that Todd was silent, it was up to him to speak—and he still didn't have anything to say.

"I'm waiting," Todd said impatiently. "C'mon, Watts, spill."

Tom scrambled for a delaying tactic. That was it! He'd put Todd on the defensive. "Before I say anything more," Tom said seriously, "I'd like to know what you're planning."

"What do you mean?" It had worked. Todd was definitely on the defensive.

"I just need to make sure you're really on my side before I tell you what I found out about Burgess," Tom said authoritatively.

"I'm on Elizabeth's side," Todd replied stiffly.

"OK." Tom nodded. "So, tell me your plans."

Todd crossed his arms over his chest and stared at Tom. "How can I tell you about my plans when I don't even know what I'm supposed to be planning!"

Tom crossed his arms over his chest in imitation of Todd and returned his steely glare. "Well,

I'm not going to tell you my information if you don't tell me your plans."

The two guys held their ground for a full minute before Todd finally dropped his arms. "You didn't hear anything, did you, Watts?"

Tom dropped his arms and shook his head regretfully. "So, what are we going to do? We can't just let that slime continue to play around with Elizabeth!" *Besides*, he added silently, *I need her back in my arms. And time's running out.*

"That was pretty hairy," Ruby said as she sipped a cup of coffee. "Didn't you think so, Elizabeth?"

"You mean riding up to the top or looking down at the ocean?" Elizabeth asked as she took an almond croissant from the buffet table. She tried to smile, but she was still smarting over Sam's rejection.

She felt herself blushing in humiliation as she caught a glimpse of him talking to one of the guys from another team.

"Hey, the bike ride was no picnic," Ruby said with a wry smile. "But I was thinking of staring down into that abyss. Are we really going to jump off the cliff tomorrow?"

"I guess we have to if we want to win," Elizabeth said absently. She couldn't forget the way Sam had looked at her when he told her he had other plans.

Why do you care so much? she asked herself in disgust. *It's pretty obvious he's not interested in you! As soon as he leaves here, he'll probably head for the nearest phone and call that girl he used to go out with!*

"You look like you're about to challenge someone to a boxing match." Ruby laughed as she gestured at Elizabeth's clenched fists.

Elizabeth unclenched her fists. "I guess I'm feeling a little bruised," she said quietly.

"Let me guess." Ruby nodded toward Sam. "What did Sam do?"

"It's more what he didn't do," Elizabeth said bitterly. "He didn't accept my dinner invitation."

Ruby's eyes widened. "You asked him out to dinner?"

"Yup."

"Girl," Ruby said sympathetically, "you've got it bad."

"Tell me about it." Elizabeth absently brushed a stray crumb off her jeans. "But you know what, Ruby?" she added, looking up and forcing a smile. "I want to enjoy the last couple of days of this competition."

"Hey," Charlie said, joining them. "What's going on?"

"Sam again," Ruby explained. "Elizabeth's down, and we're going to find a way to cheer her up. Find something to distract her."

"Right." Charlie nodded.

183

"You want to visit Hemingway's house, Elizabeth?" Ruby asked.

Elizabeth considered Ruby's suggestion. She'd been planning to visit Hemingway's house right after the training session, but suddenly the idea of a guided tour didn't seem very appealing. "How about something a little more exciting?" she said. "What about snorkeling? There are lots of gorgeous coral reefs and tropical fish. . . ."

"Sounds like fun," Charlie agreed enthusiastically.

"I'm up for it," Ruby seconded.

"Snorkeling? Do you mind if I tag along?" Alisha Korn said as she passed by with a croissant and coffee.

"Sure," Elizabeth said with an easy smile.

Charlie squeezed Elizabeth's shoulder. "I'm going to get Scott and tell him. I'll catch up with you."

"Hey, Elizabeth, Alisha, Ruby." Danny Wyatt joined the girls as Charlie took off. "Anyone interested in a glass-bottomed boat tour?"

"Sorry, Danny," Alisha said. "We're all going snorkeling."

"That sounds cool. Do you mind if I come?"

Elizabeth smiled at Danny. "Of course not."

Within a few minutes word of Elizabeth's expedition had circulated and a crowd of almost twenty people joined the plan.

"Let's head down to the beach now," Elizabeth said. "We can rent equipment there."

She turned and started to walk off.

She was glad so many people had decided to go snorkeling. What she wasn't happy about was the fact that Sam was part of the crowd.

So much for trying to distract myself!

Chapter
Ten

"This is too fabulous!" Jessica exclaimed, holding up a night-light made from a giant conch shell. "It would look so awesome in my dorm room. Of course, it's not as fabulous as that mother-of-pearl inlaid picture frame you swiped from under my nose back in Savannah," she pouted. "But it's still pretty good. What do you think, Neil?"

"It's OK." Neil shrugged. "But I like this better." He pointed to a paperweight made from a small, petrified octopus.

Jessica swatted him with her purse. "Don't be silly!" She couldn't remember the last time she'd had so much fun. She and Neil had spent the last twenty minutes wandering in and out of the more offbeat shops in Old Town. Neil was the perfect shopping companion. He had even better taste than Lila, but unlike Lila, he didn't mind carrying Jessica's packages. Jessica couldn't believe she'd been denying herself such a great buddy for the past weeks.

Neil's right, she told herself. *It was stupid for me to get all bent out of shape just because he's not interested in me as a woman. He's as much fun and as much of a gentleman as Elvis!*

"What are you thinking about?" Neil asked. "You looked pretty serious there for a second."

Jessica smiled. "I was just thinking that you're right."

Neil quirked an eyebrow. "You mean that the petrified octopus is a better buy than the conch night-light?"

"No!" Jessica laughed. "That isn't what I meant. I just was thinking that it was pretty silly for me to be mad at you," Jessica said, her cheeks flushing a delicate shade of rose.

Neil took her arm and shepherded her out of the store. "I'm right about a lot of things."

"Is that so, Mr. Martin?"

"Yes, it is," Neil said confidently. "And I have more words of wisdom for you. But let's get lunch first. I'm starving. You raced away after the training session so quickly, I didn't have time to grab anything from the buffet."

"I can't wait to hear your new words of wisdom," Jessica grumbled as they walked into a small, dark restaurant. Fishing nets decorated the walls, and the floor was covered with a fine coating of sand. "So, let me hear them," she whined as she slid into one of the booths and picked up a menu.

"How does Cajun conch sound?" Neil asked, peering over his menu.

"Repulsive," Jessica replied with a tinge of impatience. "Neil, c'mon, what do you have to tell me?"

"Should I just go with a burger, then?" Neil mused. He frowned as he scanned the chalkboard that rested against the far wall. On it were printed the day's specials. "I'm so tired of burgers, though."

"Neil! Tell me!" Jessica protested. She ripped the menu out of his hand and signaled the waitress. "Two burgers with fries and a couple of iced teas, please," she said. The waitress scooped up their menus and left. Jessica steepled her hands under her chin and regarded Neil sternly. "Spill, OK?"

"OK." Neil nodded easily. "You're scared of jumping tomorrow."

Jessica stared. "That's supposed to be news? Words of wisdom? Big deal! Anybody could have told you that I'm scared of jumping off that cliff!"

"Yeah, maybe, but here's the interesting part," Neil said. "If you don't jump tomorrow, you're only screwing yourself."

"No, you mean I'm saving myself," Jessica corrected. "I could break a leg jumping. Or worse!" She gulped nervously.

"I don't think so." Neil leaned forward and fixed her with his deep gray eyes. "Look, Jessica, I joined this whole competition thing to cash in, but that doesn't look like it's going to happen now." Neil paused as the waitress set their drinks down on the table. "Oh, sure, we could pull out of last place tomorrow, but it's mathematically impossible that we'll be able to snag the big prize." He paused and took a sip of his iced tea.

"All the more reason to bail," Jessica muttered as she fiddled with her silverware.

"Uh-uh," Neil went on. "Don't you see? I started on this trip to win, but it's turned into something much more for me. And for you too, I think."

"What do you mean?" Jessica frowned at him.

"I mean that I've changed this summer, and so have you. I've learned to face up to a lot of different things."

"I've changed?" Jessica looked surprised. "Well, I guess you're right," she said slowly. "But what does that have to do with jumping off a cliff?"

"Everything," Neil said. "It's the ultimate challenge. The ultimate test. Look, Jessica, I'm scared to do it too. So is everyone, but that's the point. This whole contest has been about coming to terms with your fears." Neil nodded thoughtfully. "I tell you, Jessica, I never thought I'd say this, but I got a lot more out of this summer than I thought I would. It doesn't matter if I go home broke."

"Are you crazy?" Jessica yelped. "What could you possibly have learned that could take the place of money?" she demanded.

"I learned how to look a straight woman in the eye and tell her I'm gay," Neil said simply. "Before this summer I was always too afraid to do that. I always figured that I'd be rejected as a person."

"Oh, Neil, I'm so sorry," Jessica whispered. She reached across the table and grabbed his hand. Her eyes misted over as she thought of how much she must have hurt him. *I never thought about what it must have been like for him!* She increased the pressure on Neil's hand. *I was only thinking of my own feelings.*

"But don't you see, Jess? You did reject me, and I lived through it," Neil continued, shrugging. "Who knows, maybe it's time I came out of the closet to everyone."

"Maybe you should make an announcement at the wrap party tomorrow," Jessica said with a giggle. "You know, ICSN is taping the party. Ned Jackson will definitely be going around for sound bites. Can't you just see the look on the sponsors' faces!"

"Uh, maybe." Neil laughed. "But don't count on it. Tell me what *you* learned this summer."

"Hmmm." Jessica knit her brows thoughtfully. "Let's see. I learned that I'm naturally beautiful and can get away without having to wear much makeup. I learned that my fashion sense is so developed that

I can pack light and still come up with plenty of creative outfits. I've learned that being a celebrity has its downside. I've learned how to live with a whole bunch of people in a really cramped space." Jessica paused. "And I've learned how to deal when the best-looking guy I've seen in months turns out to be gay."

"Months?" Neil said indignantly.

"Well, at least three months," Jessica drawled. She ducked as Neil threw his napkin at her. "But seriously, Neil, just because I've changed doesn't mean I'm up for jumping off a cliff."

"I think it does," Neil argued. "Don't you feel right now like you're able to take on lots of new challenges? Imagine how you'll feel after you've jumped off the cliff! Like you can do absolutely anything!" Neil placed his hand on Jessica's arm. "Besides, Jessica, it will be fun. I'll hold your hand, and we'll take a running leap from the edge together."

"Maybe." Jessica nodded slowly. "You're right. I never thought I'd be able to handle a lot of the things thrown my way this summer," she said, nervously pleating her napkin. *But I did,* she realized.

"OK. I'll do it. But on one condition!" she said firmly, looking Neil straight in the eye.

Neil grinned. "No problem."

"If I jump off the cliff, if I risk my life just to prove I can handle challenges, I deserve something very, very special."

"Sure, anything." Neil shrugged. "What do you want?"

"The mother-of-pearl inlaid picture frame," Jessica said triumphantly.

"How do you put this on?" Uli looked at Sam quizzically. He held his snorkel upside down and his mask was draped crookedly around his neck. "We do not have such things in Sweden," he said as he attempted to untangle his mask.

"It's not hard. Just do what I do." Sam put on his own mask and adjusted the snorkel to fit his mouth. "You see?" he said, his voice sounding strange through the apparatus. "Nothing to it." He whipped the snorkel out of his mouth and tossed his mask down on the sand.

Sam really had no interest in snorkeling. Sticking a rubber hose in his mouth so he could check out some seaweed at close range wasn't his idea of fun. But he *was* interested in sticking close to Elizabeth. The argument with Josh had been the last straw. It had made him realize just how stupidly he'd been behaving the past few weeks. What a coward he'd been. He liked Elizabeth. A lot. He wanted to see if something could happen between them. The problem was that after the lousy way he'd been treating her, he had no idea how to reapproach her.

Should he just apologize to Elizabeth? he wondered. Or should he be more forceful, act like he hadn't rejected her earlier and tell her that he'd changed his mind about dinner?

Sam glanced down the beach to where Elizabeth stood laughing with Ruby and Charlie. His heart twisted at how beautiful and carefree she looked.

"Is something wrong, Sam?" Uli asked as he smeared a generous amount of sunblock on his fair skin. "You have a most unhappy expression on your face."

"Yeah, something's wrong, all right," Sam muttered unhappily. "I've done something really stupid, and I think it may be too late to fix my mistake." He watched as Elizabeth waded out into the water, laughing and splashing with Ruby and some of the guys from Team Four. Sam frowned as he saw Tom and Todd skulking a few feet away from her. *What is with those guys?* he thought angrily. *They're acting like they're on some covert spy mission or something.* Todd bumped into Tom, and Sam grinned. *Correction*, he thought. *They look like Tweedledum and Tweedledee.*

"Stupid?" Uli frowned. "You mean when you messed up in the Civil War event?"

"No," Sam said shortly.

"Oh, you mean when you spit tobacco juice all over Elizabeth?"

"No," Sam replied, struggling to keep his voice even.

"Then you mean when you laughed at Elizabeth when she—"

"Uli!" Sam restrained himself from wringing his neck. "I mean that I really like Elizabeth, but I've been totally nasty to her, and I think that it might be too late to fix things."

"It's not too late, definitely not," Uli said, bobbing his head for emphasis.

"How do you know?" Sam asked. He sat down on his towel and watched as Elizabeth disappeared beneath the water. And then he noticed that instead of following her, Wilkins and Watts seemed to have their sights pinned on him. *With all the cute girls on this beach they can't find something better to look at?* Sam grinned. He turned his attention back to Uli. He was much more interested in what Uli had to say than in trying to figure out what went on in the minds of the Preppy Twins.

"I just know," Uli went on. "Look, Elizabeth is a most fair girl. You see the way she behaves whenever anyone has an argument. She always tries to see every side, yes?"

"Yeah, so?" Sam said, unconvinced.

"So, she is going to listen to you. She would listen to anyone who apologized to her, but especially to you, Sam."

Sam looked at Uli in surprise. "But why?"

Uli smiled. "Believe me, sometimes when she thinks no one is watching, she is looking at you with a very special expression on her face."

"Really?" Sam felt pleased.

"Really. I say you should go to her." Uli gave

Sam a friendly shove. "Go on, and tell me later what happens." Uli paused as if considering whether to go ahead and say what he wanted to say. "And Sam," he added gently, "maybe you should not be talking things over with Josh so much either."

Sam smiled ruefully. "Hey, that party's over," he said as he picked up his mask and got to his feet.

"What party?" Uli asked.

"It's just an expression. I mean that I won't be confiding in Josh anymore." Sam clapped Uli on the shoulder. "OK, wish me luck, pal. I'm going after her."

Sam pulled his mask over his head as he sprinted toward the shore. He stopped at the waterline and adjusted his snorkel. He was so focused on going after Elizabeth, he didn't notice the way Tom and Todd were still staring at him and nudging each other.

Here goes, buddy, Sam thought as he waded out into deeper water. Finally he took a deep breath and plunged in.

Even though Sam didn't have a high opinion of snorkeling, it was hard not to be impressed by the spectacular sights he found underwater. Schools of brightly colored fish swam by rosy-colored coral reefs. Sea anemones were blooming everywhere, and Sam thought he saw a small octopus dart beneath a rock.

But as dazzling as the underwater sights were, they couldn't compete with the vision Elizabeth made as she swam several yards away in a bright purple bikini.

Sam kicked his flippers and turned in her direction. But before he'd swum five feet, he was suddenly stopped by the massive figure of Tom Watts, treading water, less than a foot in front of him.

What the— Sam kicked his legs to turn away. No sooner had he gotten past Tom's roadblock than Todd Wilkins appeared like an avenging angel. Sam kicked and used his arms in a breaststroke to turn 180—and swam right into Tom! Sam whipped to the right, but so did Wilkins. No matter what direction he chose, Wilkins and Watts blocked his way!

Sam lowered his head and shoulders to dive deeper, but like perfectly synchronized water-ballet dancers, Tom and Todd flipped over and under him.

Frantically Sam kicked hard with his flippers and swam past Tom to the surface. He ripped off his snorkel and gasped for breath. "What's with those weirdos?" he spluttered. "Are they trying to snorkel or play defense for the Chicago Bulls?"

Angrily Sam swam back to shore. He realized it didn't really matter what game Wilkins and Watts were playing. What mattered was that they had prevented him from getting close to Elizabeth. And what mattered even more was that he still hadn't apologized to her.

"Forget it," Sam muttered disgustedly. Obviously he wasn't meant to be with a girl as wonderful as Elizabeth. It just wasn't meant to happen. He climbed out of the water and trudged up the beach toward his towel.

"Are you sure it's safe for you to go swimming?" Scott asked anxiously.

"Of course it's OK." Charlie smiled down at him as he lay stretched out on the big blue beach towel they shared. "What could possibly go wrong?" she asked, reaching into her tote bag for a tube of sunblock. She began applying the thick white cream to Scott's back.

"Mmmm, that feels good," Scott murmured appreciatively. He flipped over suddenly and stared at Charlie with a serious expression on his face. "Couldn't something go wrong?" he asked. "I mean, I don't know, but are you really sure it's safe?"

"You mean, am I sure that my snorkel will work? Or do you mean, is it dangerous to go swimming because I'm pregnant?" Charlie asked with a touch of impatience as she screwed the cap back on the tube of sunblock and tossed it into her bag.

"I mean because you're pregnant," Scott said quietly.

Charlie couldn't stay mad at Scott for long. Not when he was just being overprotective. Ever since Scott had joined the group the day before, he'd been treating her as if she were as fragile as the finest crystal.

And to think I was so worried about how he'd react to the news, Charlie thought mistily. Although Scott had been supportive on the phone, until yesterday they hadn't seen each other since she'd told him she was pregnant. Charlie had been afraid that Scott wouldn't be so understanding in person. But Scott had been even more tender toward her than ever before.

"Well?" Scott persisted. "Do you think you'll be OK if we go in the water? Will, uh . . . will the baby be OK?"

"Of course!" Charlie ruffled his hair. "Look, Scott, if I can jump off a cliff, then I can go snorkeling."

"That's true," Scott said slowly, fiddling with his mask. "But who says that you should go jumping off the cliff tomorrow? What if something happens then?"

"I'm going to jump tomorrow, Scott," Charlie said firmly. She took a deep breath. "I learned a lot this summer. I learned not to be so timid. I learned to face down my fears." She looked deep into his eyes. "I guess what I'm saying is that I *want* to jump tomorrow. Besides, it would be totally unfair to the rest of the team to bail now. It looks like we might pull off first prize, and if I don't jump, then we'll be automatically disqualified."

"I guess you're right." Scott sighed regretfully. "I figured that you'd stick by your team."

"Just like I figured that you'd stick by me," Charlie said quietly.

"Of course I would." Scott reached for her hand. "Did you ever doubt it?"

"No, I didn't." Charlie shook her head emphatically. "But it's just such a big thing we're facing. A baby . . . I guess I was a little scared. I *am* a little scared," she corrected.

"Me too," Scott admitted. "But you know what? We both learned a lot this summer. You learned not to be so timid. And I learned more than ever how much I love you. We can get through this, Charlie."

"I know we can." Charlie swallowed a lump in her throat and blinked back a few tears. "It's kind of funny, isn't it? My parents thought that if they made me go on this trip, it would break us up. Instead we just got that much closer."

"Nothing could ever make me break up with you," Scott said huskily. "And even though we don't know what we're going to do about our situation, I know that I'll always love you."

"You'd better stop, or I'll really start crying!" Charlie laughed and brushed her hand across her eyes. "C'mon, let's go swimming!"

"High five, dude!" Todd laughed triumphantly as he treaded water and held up his hand. It was hard to stay afloat with one hand in the air, but he was in such a good mood, he didn't care. "Thanks to my brilliant idea, we actually managed to accomplish something! We kept Sam from going anywhere near Elizabeth!"

Tom shook the water out of his hair and slapped Todd's hand. "We were awesome!" he shouted. "Did you see the look on Burgess's face when he realized he couldn't get by us?"

"It was hysterical!" Todd removed his mask and continued to tread water. "I thought I was going to die laughing."

Todd couldn't believe they'd actually been able to thwart Sam's plans to get close to Elizabeth. After Tom had come back from his reconnaissance mission on the mountain empty-handed, Todd didn't know what to do. How were they going to stop Sam from spending time with Elizabeth? But Elizabeth herself had provided the solution when she suggested the trip to the beach. It was clear from the look on Sam's face as he'd trailed after her that he was up to something. Todd had decided he and Tom should follow along and find out exactly what.

Of course, I couldn't have foiled Sam's plans without Watts, Todd admitted. There'd been one point when he was sure Sam was going to get away. But then Tom had been there to block him. *It never hurts to have a former quarterback on your side,* Todd thought with a grin.

"And the way that he tried to dive under us," Tom went on as he removed his own mask. "I don't know what kind of stunt he thought he was pulling."

"Well, we definitely kept him away from Elizabeth," Todd said. "Maybe now that he knows we're watching out for her, he'll stay away. Hey, what's with you?" Todd frowned at the strange faces Tom was making. "You look like you've seen a ghost. Did you swallow too much salt water or something? What are you pointing at?"

"I, uh . . . um. Hi, Elizabeth," Tom said weakly.

Todd whipped around.

And then he considered giving himself a dunking. The look on Elizabeth's face was not pleasant.

"Hey, Elizabeth," he choked out. "What's going on?"

"Why don't you tell me, Todd." Elizabeth's eyes flashed fire as she removed her mask.

"Uh, well, Tom and I, we were just . . ."

"You were just meddling in my life and treating me like a five-year-old child instead of a grown woman! Again! Not to mention the fact that you were acting like a couple of immature frat boys. Scratch that. You were acting like a couple of immature third graders!"

"We just wanted to help you," Tom said weakly.

"Help me with what?" Elizabeth asked sarcastically. "Snorkeling?"

"No, Elizabeth." Todd reached out to touch her, but Elizabeth expertly moved out of his reach. "We wanted to make sure that you didn't get hurt."

"Get hurt? You mean by a jellyfish or something? Oh, I get it," she said, slapping her forehead. "You wanted to make sure I didn't get hurt by Sam!"

"That's right, exactly," Tom said, bobbing his head up and down for emphasis.

"How dare you?" Elizabeth said, her voice icy. "Who do you think you are? My keepers? What I do or don't do with Sam Burgess isn't any of your business. Any. I've told you that before." Her face softened a fraction as she looked at Todd. "Maybe you were motivated by some incredibly misguided attempt at chivalry," she said. "I can understand your wanting to protect me if you thought Sam was bad news. But Todd, for one thing, it's not your business any longer, and for another, you could have just come to me and told me your fears."

Todd was ashamed but also slightly relieved. Elizabeth was angry with him, but he knew she'd get over it and forgive him. But Tom . . . He couldn't help feeling bad for Tom as Elizabeth turned her attention to him.

"*You* have no excuse," she growled, jabbing her finger at his chest. "What could you possibly have been thinking? That I'd be so grateful you'd rescued me from Sam, I'd come rushing back into your arms?" Tom didn't answer. Todd thought his friend looked slightly green with shame. "I have one thing to say to you, Tom. Get real, get over it, and get a life!" Elizabeth gave both of them one last disgusted look before striking out toward shore.

Todd turned to look at Tom. "Whose stupid idea was this anyway?" he said lamely.

Jessica hummed a little tune as she walked down Whitehead Street in the direction of her hotel. She'd had a fabulous day playing with Neil, but now that he had gone off to catch a movie, she was feeling a little tired. She just wanted to take a bubble bath and order room service like Todd had suggested the night before.

I'm so wiped, I bet I'll fall asleep as soon as my head touches the pillow, she thought as she swung her many shopping bags back and forth. *I can't wait to try . . .* "Elizabeth!" Jessica yelled as she saw her sister disappear around the corner. "Hey, Elizabeth, wait up!"

Elizabeth turned, startled, but her whole face lit up when she saw who it was running toward her. "Jess!" she cried. She ran toward her twin, arms stretched wide.

"How are you? Where were you just now? Are you psyched about tomorrow? I feel like I haven't really talked to you in forever! Not alone anyway.

Not since Chicago." The words tumbled out of Jessica's mouth as she hugged her twin sister.

"Hold up." Elizabeth laughed as she pulled away from Jessica. "First, a bunch of us went snorkeling. And then I checked out Hemingway's house. What have *you* been doing? Oh, let me guess—shopping?"

"A little," Jessica said coyly, falling into step beside Elizabeth. All of a sudden she felt energized, and her desire for a bath and bed were completely forgotten. Now what she wanted to do was stay up all night and talk to her sister. "Do you want to have dinner together?" she asked Elizabeth hopefully. "Or do you have to hang with your team?"

Elizabeth smiled. "Nope, I'm free, and you know something? There's nothing I'd rather do than go to one of those really nice restaurants on Duval Street and have a great dinner with you."

"Let's do it," Jessica said as she dragged Elizabeth around the corner and in the direction of Duval Street.

"So, are you scared about tomorrow?" Elizabeth asked as they walked along the crowded, early evening sidewalk. "I know I am."

"Well, sure I'm scared. But I'm also looking forward to it," Jessica said confidently. "I was thinking about bailing, but Neil talked me out of it."

"Somebody managed to talk you out of something?" Elizabeth's eyes widened in surprise. "I've got to hear this one—and I'm dying to know all about Neil. He's gorgeous! Did things work out between you the way you wanted them to?"

"Well, not exactly," Jessica said, her expression suddenly shuttered. *Should I tell Elizabeth that Neil's gay?* she wondered. *Nah,* she decided. *It's his life. He'll tell people when he wants them to know.* "What I want to know is what went on between you and Sam," Jessica said brightly. "Whenever I've seen you two together, there's been a really strange vibe in the air."

"Tell me about it." Elizabeth rolled her eyes. "Oh, wait. How about this place?" she asked, stopping outside an elegant restaurant.

"Looks great," Jessica said as she glanced at the menu displayed on a stand just outside the front window. She peered in at the small, candlelit room festooned with great bunches of flowers in porcelain vases. "I haven't been to a place like this since the last time I went out to dinner with Lila in Sweet Valley," she said excitedly. "Good thing I'm wearing one of the new dresses I bought this afternoon!"

"And I'm glad I changed into this long skirt before I came into town. But I don't know, Jess," Elizabeth teased. "I'm not sure Le Chat Noir can compete with lukewarm leftovers served in the back of a Winnebago!" She followed Jessica inside.

"So, tell me everything about what's going

on with Sam," Jessica said as they were shown to a small, round table by the front window. She sat down and spread her linen napkin on her lap. "And not just with Sam either. Tell me everything that's been going on with everybody!"

Elizabeth fiddled with the two pretty yellow roses in a small vase on their table. "Well, I didn't get along so well with Ruby and Charlie at first." She paused and shook her head with a laugh. "I thought you were hard to live with, Jess, but at least you're my twin. It's hard sharing a small space with people you're not close to."

"Who says I'm hard to live with?" Jessica squawked.

Elizabeth raised an eyebrow.

"Anyway, go on," Jessica urged.

"I've really grown to like them," Elizabeth said slowly. "They each have such a different perspective on life." Elizabeth frowned slightly, and she took her hand away from the roses. "I've learned a lot from them. Ruby's so carefree, and Charlie is really strong in her own way. I don't think I'll ever be just like Ruby or Charlie, but I do think they each helped me to loosen up a bit."

"Really?" Jessica sat back in her chair. "You mean, you won't be making your bed with hospital corners anymore?"

"Ha ha," Elizabeth said sarcastically as she flipped open her menu. "Why don't we talk about *you* for a while?"

"OK," Jessica said agreeably. "But you still haven't told me about Sam. You have to promise to tell me all about him over dessert."

"I promise. And I'm going to have the swordfish." Elizabeth closed her menu and leaned closer to Jessica. "It's your turn. C'mon, tell me about Neil."

"I'll have the swordfish too." Jessica smiled as the waiter approached. "OK, forget Neil for a second. I have to tell you it was the worst moment of my life when I found out I was going to be stuck living with both your exes for the summer!"

Elizabeth laughed as Jessica placed their orders. "I can only imagine," she gasped after the waiter had walked away. "Wait until you hear about the stunt they pulled today. They are determined to keep me and Sam apart."

Jessica frowned. "Those two guys have been jumping out of their skins since they realized there might be something between you and Sam. What did they do today? Let the air out of Sam's bike tires so he couldn't ride after you up the mountain?"

"Something like that." Elizabeth sighed. "Tell me what Pam and Rob are like."

"Ha! Your exes are nothing compared to them. I swear, they're the most nauseating couple that ever existed."

"Sounds like you've had a hard time,"

Elizabeth said sympathetically as she reached for the bread basket.

"Actually," Jessica said, "I've had a great time this summer. OK, I'm not too happy about being in last place, but other than that, the trip has been a blast." Jessica sat up straighter in her chair. She couldn't believe what she'd just said, but it was really true. In spite of Tom and Todd's antics, in spite of the fact that Pam and Rob were too awful for words, and even in spite of the fact that Neil had turned her down, she'd had a really fabulous summer.

"I guess that means Neil turned out to be even more wonderful than you thought he'd be," Elizabeth said with a grin.

"He did," Jessica said honestly.

"Is it serious?" Elizabeth asked, her voice low.

Jessica smiled. "As serious as it can be. But we're just friends. Maybe we're even on the way to being best friends, but nothing else is going to happen."

Elizabeth's jaw dropped. "Is this Jessica Wakefield I'm talking to? Have aliens stolen your soul or something? C'mon, Jess, 'just friends'? That's not what you were after when you asked me to switch teams at the beginning of the trip, and you know it!"

Jessica shrugged. "Things change."

"It sounds like *you've* changed," Elizabeth said in amazement.

Their dinner arrived, and Jessica dug into her swordfish. "So, OK, we did me. Let's get back to Sam."

"It's not dessert yet!" Elizabeth protested. "Oh, OK." She sighed. "He's not like any other guy I've ever been interested in. You know how Tom and Todd are so—"

"Dull and boring?" Jessica interrupted.

"Try responsible and considerate," Elizabeth corrected. "Well, Sam's the opposite. He can be really sarcastic and really moody. And then he can be so sweet and romantic and helpful. You never know where you are with him. I don't know where I am with him now, except that I know I really like him, and I think he likes me. Only I'm not sure."

"So, what are you going to do?" Jessica asked.

Elizabeth toyed with her food. "I don't know, Jess. Tomorrow's the last day of the trip. I don't see how we could work everything out by then." She shrugged and looked at her sister. "I'm not going to worry about it, though. Whatever happens, happens."

"Hello, is this Elizabeth Wakefield I'm talking to?" Jessica said. "Have aliens stolen *your* soul or something? You always have a plan and a schedule for everything! I can't believe you're being so laid-back about this."

"I guess we've both changed," Elizabeth said. "You know what, Jess? I think we got way more than we bargained for when we signed up for this competition."

Jessica looked at Elizabeth in the flickering candlelight. "I know what you mean," she said with a smile. "And something tells me that when we go back to Sweet Valley, our lives will have been changed forever."

Chapter Eleven

"Listen up, guys, and listen well!" Richie Valentine stood on a small, makeshift platform at the bottom of the hill as the ICSN Coast-to-Coast competitors clustered around him. At the previous events Richie had had to ask for quiet several times before everyone tuned in to his announcements. But today the members of Teams One, Two, Three, and Four went silent immediately and stood white-faced, hanging on his every word.

That's because they're all so scared, Sam thought as he grasped the handlebars on his bike. His own heart was pounding against his ribs, but that wasn't because he was so frightened about the up-coming event. It was because he was so nervous about what he wanted to say to Elizabeth. He glanced over at her, but even though she was only a few feet away, she seemed completely unaware that he was staring at her.

He swallowed hard as he took in her drawn, pale face. *Does she look that way because she's nervous?* he wondered. *Or because she thinks that I spent the night in another woman's arms?*

"Now, this event is real simple," Richie continued. "It doesn't take much skill, just stamina and courage. All you have to do is get up that mountain as fast as you can, drop your bike, then close your eyes and take a running leap. The first team to get all of its members into the water wins. So, listen up for the starting gun—and may the best team win!"

Sam barely heard the announcer's words. He was too busy trying to edge his bike closer to Elizabeth's. He was sure she would be able to hear the thumping of his heart as he approached, but Elizabeth didn't notice him until he was right beside her. She glanced at him and then quickly looked away, but not before Sam saw the hurt in her eyes. He had a sudden urge to kick himself.

"Elizabeth," he said quietly. A single blond curl had escaped her ponytail, and he brushed it aside. Elizabeth jumped as if she had been burned. She turned to face him, and this time there were sparks shooting from her eyes.

"Elizabeth, just give me a second," Sam said hurriedly. "I know how you must feel. I've been a total jerk the whole summer. I wish I had gone out to dinner with you last night, but I was too scared. I spent the evening alone. I never called my ex. She's just a bad memory." He paused to take a deep breath and was relieved to see the beginnings of a small smile dawning on Elizabeth's face.

"Will you give me another chance, Elizabeth?" Sam asked softly.

Elizabeth opened her mouth to answer. "Well, I . . ."

Bang! The starter gun popped, and the air was filled with the sound of dozens of spinning wheels.

The final event had officially begun.

Jessica leaped on her bike and pedaled as fast as she could. Her mind was totally focused on getting to the top of the mountain, and she was glad to see that her teammates seemed as determined as she was. Maybe it was because it was their last chance; maybe they were just better cyclists than everyone else. Jessica didn't know. But she did know that her team was really pulling together.

Tom and Todd led the pack with Neil right behind them. Rob and Pam were a little bit behind her, but still, they were pedaling for all they were worth.

We're going to make it! Jessica exulted. *We're going to win this event!* She leaned over the handlebars, her face growing red with the effort of riding up the steep incline.

The breeze whipped her hair around her face and partially obscured her vision, making it difficult to negotiate the bumpy trail. She could feel sweat beginning to bead at her temples and her calves were screaming for mercy, but nothing deterred her.

"We're going to make it," she chanted through gritted teeth. "We're going to be the first group to hit the water."

Jessica squeezed every last breath from her exhausted lungs. She was riding on pure adrenaline, and she didn't know how much longer she could keep up the intensity.

"I've got to . . . *oh!*" Jessica screeched to an awkward halt and was tossed against her handlebars. A sharp pebble had struck and cut through her front tire.

"No!" she wailed as the air began to seep out of the tire. "This isn't happening!"

"Jessica!" Rob cried as he and then Pam cycled by. "C'mon!"

"I can't!"

"Jessica!"

It was Neil, racing back down the hill. He slammed to a stop by her damaged bike. "C'mon, we're still ahead of the rest of the pack. We can win this thing! Jump on my handlebars."

Jessica dropped her own bike and jumped on Neil's handlebars. Together they turned back up the mountain. "Lucky you were already more than halfway through with the course," he puffed. "I don't think I could have made it all the way up the mountain like this."

"Keep pedaling!" Jessica urged.

They reached the top. "Let's go!" Neil cried, exhaustion clear in his voice. Jessica jumped off the handlebars and Neil threw the bike down as they raced to the edge. The rest of the team was already standing there, breathless and scared.

"C'mon!" Jessica cried excitedly. "We're the first full team up here. We can scoop this event, but we gotta go now!" Quickly she looked down the mountain. The other teams were gaining on them fast. It was only a matter of seconds before they would join Team One at the cliff's edge.

"Let's hold hands and take a running leap," Jessica ordered.

"You got it!" Todd cried.

Team One clasped hands and looked at each other nervously as they backed up a few steps.

"OK, on the count of three." Jessica was so excited, she could barely breathe. "And guys? Whatever happens, it's been a great summer. OK. Let's do it."

"One! Two! Three!"

The air was filled with screams as Team One ran over the edge of the cliff and plunged fifty feet into the sparkling turquoise water below.

Elizabeth jumped off her bike and raced to the edge of the cliff. *I can't do this,* she realized. Sweat broke out on her forehead, and she reared back at the sight of the fifty-foot drop.

"Yeah, you can." Sam came up behind her and whispered in her ear, "We can do it together. C'mon." He grabbed her hand and walked back several paces. "You ready?"

Elizabeth swallowed hard. Her stomach was a mass of knots and butterflies. She was beyond scared, but she also knew that she had to jump in the water *now*. Teams One and Three had already gone over the edge, and the members of Team Four were about to jump. *At least Sam's holding my hand,* she thought as she glanced down at his strong, suntanned arm.

"OK." Her smile was grim. "Let's do it."

Sam looked intensely at her. "I'm going to count to three, and then we'll just run, OK?" he said, his voice tight with anxiety.

Elizabeth tightened her grip on his hand. "OK. But Sam, before we jump, I just want to tell you one thing." She looked up at him and felt her heart expand. "I'm really glad you didn't call your ex-girlfriend."

He gave her a small smile. "Me too. Now, one . . ."

"Two," Elizabeth gasped.

"Three!" Elizabeth closed her eyes as they raced to the edge. The moment she realized there was no ground beneath her, her eyes flew open.

"Aaahhh!" she cried as she whizzed through the air and hit the deliciously refreshing water with a splash.

Elizabeth broke through the surface and shook

the water out of her eyes. "We did it!" she cried, throwing her arms around Sam. "We really did it!"

"We sure did!" Sam held Elizabeth close as other contestants splashed into the water around them.

"Have you ever had so much fun in your life?" Ruby said, laughing excitedly.

"How do you think we scored?" Charlie asked. When she saw Elizabeth in Sam's arms, she winked.

"We should find out any second," Elizabeth answered, blushing. "We should . . ." She started to speak but was cut off by Richie Valentine as he boomed into his microphone from the top of the cliff.

"Congratulations, kids, you did it! And now for the moment of truth. First we're going to announce your scores in this event and then your overall standings. Team One, first in the water. Great team spirit."

Elizabeth smiled as she saw Jessica and the rest of Team One go wild.

"But sorry, people, doubling up on the bikes is not allowed. You are *disqualified*, and you're last overall in the ICSN Coast-to-Coast competition."

"Oh, poor Jess," Elizabeth said regretfully.

"Team Two . . . ," Richie went on.

Elizabeth held her breath, and Sam squeezed her tight. Ruby and Charlie clutched each other, and Uli and Josh looked at each other tensely.

"Fourth in the water, but because Team One was disqualified, third in this event, and second overall!"

"I won three thousand dollars!" Josh yelled as everyone else whooped and hugged each other.

"Team Four, second in this event and third overall. And the winners—*Team Three,* first in this event and first overall. Now, everyone, don't forget you have one great farewell party tonight. See all you Coast-to-Coasters there."

Chapter
Twelve

"Who borrowed my hot rollers?" Alisha Korn stuck her head out of her room and yelled down the hall. "I need to set my hair."

"I think Vickie had them," Briana Fulton answered as she ran by with a mouthful of bobby pins. "Hey, does anyone have a good mask? My skin is looking really dried out. Sorry!" she cried as she bumped into Ruby. "I wasn't watching where I was going."

"Don't worry about it," Ruby said as she ducked into her room and closed the door behind her with a sigh of relief.

The hotel was overrun with the various contestants in various stages of undress, getting ready for the farewell party. The mood in the air was positively electric. It was clear that everyone—winners and losers alike—was in a totally upbeat mood.

"Everyone except me," Ruby muttered as she

threw her duffel bag on her bed and started tossing clothes into it. Ruby sighed deeply and shook her head as she folded a sweatshirt. She wasn't feeling bad, exactly. Overall she'd had a great time on the trip, and the prize money wasn't too shabby either. She was just feeling—left out.

No one will even miss me if I cut out early, Ruby thought sadly as she checked the closets to make sure that she wasn't leaving anything behind. *Everyone else is paired up. Charlie's really happy with Scott, and Elizabeth seems to have worked things out with Sam. But I'm on my own.* She stooped to pick up her guitar. *It's just me and my music, as always. And it's time for us to hit the road.*

She grabbed her duffel and, hoisting it over her shoulder, flung open the door. Charlie and Elizabeth almost fell in.

"I knew it!" Elizabeth cried. Her hair was dripping wet, and she had some kind of purple goo all over her face. "I knew you'd try and escape at the last minute!"

Charlie's face was also covered in purple goo. "Weren't you even going to say good-bye?" she demanded.

"I . . . wha . . . How did you know?" Ruby stammered.

"Oh, c'mon, Ruby the Loner," Elizabeth said as she pushed Ruby back into the room. "Give me some credit. I knew what you were thinking. You figure that because Charlie has Scott and I might possibly be working things out with Sam, there's no place for you."

"Well, you're wrong," Charlie said firmly.

"Didn't the three of us have a great time this summer?" Elizabeth asked as she plopped down on the bed.

"Don't you want to go to the party and celebrate?" Charlie said.

"We *did* have a great time," Ruby said slowly. "But who am I supposed to go with. Josh?"

Elizabeth laughed. "You go with us, silly."

"That's right." Charlie nodded. "We came to your room so we could all get beautiful together."

"You call that purple goo beautiful?" Ruby raised her eyebrows, but she put down her guitar case and sat on the bed next to Elizabeth.

"Goo?" Elizabeth repeated as if she was insulted. "I'll have you know that I borrowed this from my sister, Jessica, who got it from her friend Lila, who got it from Paris. It's got seaweed extract in it or something. It's supposed to make your pores glow."

"Are you sure you don't mean it's supposed to shrink your pores and make your complexion glow?" Ruby asked as Elizabeth stood and began to apply the mask to Ruby's skin.

Elizabeth shrugged. "Whatever."

"Sit still," Charlie complained as she attacked Ruby's wild mane with a brush and pins. "Boy, it's a good thing we got here when we did," she said to Elizabeth.

"You mean because we got here just in time to stop her from leaving?" Elizabeth asked.

"Uh-uh." Charlie shook her head. "I mean that it's going to take me forever to get these tangles out."

Ruby sat quietly as Elizabeth and Charlie went to work on her hair and face. She couldn't help feeling a little warm glow inside.

I didn't just make some cash this summer, she thought mistily. *I made some friends too.*

Tom snagged a drink from the bar and walked over to where Todd was standing in the far corner of the room. He really didn't have much to say to Todd anymore, but he didn't know what else to do. Pam and Rob were practically soldered together on the dance floor—not that he wanted to talk to them anyway—Jessica was busy with Neil, and Danny was dancing with Alisha Korn.

"Who else is there for me to talk to?" Tom muttered as he narrowly avoided one of the ICSN crew, setting up lights for a live broadcast of the party.

"Hey, Todd," Tom said. "So, what do you think of the party so far?"

"It's just getting started," Todd said, sitting down at one of the small tables that dotted the room. "It looks like it's going to be pretty good, though."

"I guess," Tom said quietly, sitting down next to Todd at the table.

"What's with you?" Todd asked. "I've seen people on their way to calculus midterms look happier."

"I guess I'm just feeling kind of low," Tom shouted over the music that suddenly blasted out over the loudspeakers.

"Why? Because we came in last place?" Todd shook his head ruefully. "I could have really used the cash. What am I going to do with a gift certificate to some boring housewares store?"

"It's not that. It's Elizabeth," Tom said, his eyes drifting to where she had just walked in with Sam. His heart turned over at how beautiful she looked. "I know you think that I should be over her, but c'mon, you went out with her. You know the Wakefield magic."

"Elizabeth's special, all right," Todd agreed easily. He swatted a balloon that was floating by and smiled at Tom. "This setup kind of reminds me of a high-school dance. I remember all the crazy stuff we used to do in high school. Well, Elizabeth never did crazy stuff. Although she used to cover for Jessica a lot, and she got into jams because of that." Todd laughed. "I remember one time when she . . ."

Tom stared at Todd as he launched into a long story about the Wakefield twins. It was clear that Todd had real feelings for Elizabeth. It was also clear that he'd moved on. He'd relegated Elizabeth to the past, where she belonged. To

Todd she was a cherished memory, not a continuing source of anguish.

Tom glanced over at Elizabeth again. There was no mistaking the glow in her eyes as she looked at Sam. *Maybe Elizabeth should just be a cherished memory for me too,* Tom thought as he swallowed a lump in his throat.

"You know what I think you need?" Todd asked, eyeing Tom shrewdly.

Tom turned back to him. "What?"

"I think you need to have a good time," Todd said. He stood, pulled Tom from his chair, and steered him toward Briana Fulton. "I think you need to move on."

Tom smiled at Briana. "I think you might just be right," he said. He looked at Elizabeth one last time. "It's time for me to move on."

"Want to dance?" Sam held out his hand.

Elizabeth stared at him for a moment. He looked handsomer than she had ever seen him, but she was feeling a little nervous. Things still hadn't been ironed out between them, and she had no idea what would happen after they all went home.

"Anything wrong?" he asked softly.

Elizabeth shook her head. "No. It's just that . . ."

"How about a sound bite?" Ned Jackson of the ICSN crew thrust a microphone in Elizabeth's face. She looked up, startled to find a camera trained on her. "C'mon," Jackson urged. "Give me a good quote. What did you learn this summer on the ICSN competition?"

Elizabeth looked at the camera. Then she looked back at Sam. He held out his arms, and with a small sigh she melted into them. "I learned to take each day as it comes and not worry about the future," she said, snuggling closer to Sam. "I learned how to live for the moment."

"That's great, kids," Ned Jackson said. "Can you give us a kiss or something? It would really play well."

"You bet we can," Sam said, and he lowered his mouth to Elizabeth's.

Todd grinned at the sight of Tom flailing his arms and legs as he danced circles around Briana. He looked like a giraffe to her gazelle, but he was clearly having a good time. So was Briana.

Watts isn't such a bad guy after all, Todd thought as he took a swig of his drink. *Once he learns to really get over Elizabeth, he'll be fine. I give him another five, six years to mope over her, but he'll come around.*

Todd scanned the crowd. He felt like dancing himself. He was in a pretty good mood. So, his team hadn't won anything significant. They'd had a pretty good time all in all, hadn't they?

Looks like no one's free to be my dance partner, Todd observed. *Correction. There are plenty of girls, but nobody I want to dance with. C'mon, guy, what's your problem?* he asked himself as he looked at all the beautiful women in the room. *What is it you want?*

Dana. The answer slammed into his head. Todd wanted Dana. Part of the reason he'd taken this road trip was because he was worried they were getting too serious, too fast. But the time apart had helped clear his head. He missed Dana. He wanted to be with her.

Todd reached in his pocket for his wallet and extracted a calling card. He walked swiftly to the pay phone in the corner and closed the door firmly, shutting out the noise of the dance floor. Rapidly he punched out Dana's number.

She answered on the second ring. "Hello?"

Todd closed his eyes and sighed happily at the sound of her musical voice. He felt a moment of sympathy for Watts. Elizabeth was Todd's past, but Dana was his future.

"This is wild!" Jessica yelled over the insistent beat of the music. She and Neil were dancing to some seventies-style music. "But let's sit down for a minute, OK?"

"Sure," Neil yelled back. He took her hand and dragged her off the dance floor and over to one of the small tables.

"I so need something to drink after all that," Jessica exclaimed as she brushed her hair out of her face.

"Me too." Neil collapsed into one of the chairs. He looked around the room in search of a waiter. "Is that Pam dancing with that Swedish guy from Elizabeth's team?" he asked.

Jessica nodded. "I think she had a big blowup with Rob. She's really upset they didn't pick up any money this summer, and she blames him."

Neil shuddered. "Just as long as she doesn't blame me! But I understand. I could have really used the cash too. Who needs a stupid gift certificate?"

"The rest of the team gave me their certificates," Jessica said nonchalantly.

"You can have mine too. But what do you want with them?" Neil raised his eyebrows.

"You promise I can have yours?" Jessica asked with a gleam in her eye.

Neil shrugged. "Why not? But I just can't see you buying velvet pillows and plastic napkin rings."

"Oh, you never know," Jessica replied airily.

"Whatever. But back to the money thing, Jess. I don't think my parents can scrape together another year at Stanford." Neil paused and took a deep breath. "What's SVU like?"

Jessica stared at him, openmouthed. "Are you thinking of transferring?" she whispered. Neil nodded, and she punched her fist in the air. "Yes! Awesome. We're going to have the most righteous sophomore year together!"

"Excuse me." Ned Jackson shoved a microphone at Neil. "Could you give us a sound bite for the live broadcast? We're airing as we film, so make it good. Tell us what you learned this summer."

"Tell them, Neil," Jessica said simply. "Why don't you tell everyone about the fear you conquered?"

"Perfect!" Jackson nodded. "That's the kind of thing the sponsors want. Something inspirational. Tell us about the fear you conquered this summer."

Neil looked at Jessica for a long second before turning back to the camera. "Well, I learned to get over my fear that if I came out of the closet and told everyone I was gay, no one would like me."

Ned Jackson gulped. "That's . . . that's great, son. Uh, thanks." He turned to the other members of the crew and waved them on to the next table of participants.

Jessica laughed and hugged Neil. "I'm so proud of you!" she whispered.

"Neil?" It was Tom. "Sorry, man, I couldn't help but overhear what you just said to Jackson. That takes guts. Good going." Tom stuck out his hand to shake Neil's.

"Thanks, Tom," Neil said, his eyes bright.

Todd stepped forward. "Yeah, I heard too, Neil. Hope you know this doesn't change anything. After this summer we're buds, right?"

Neil laughed. "Right."

"Cool." Todd grinned. "Look, guys, I just came to tell you I'm flying back a little early. I want to get back to Dana. So, Jess, if I don't see you back at the hotel, I'll give you my gift certificate when you get back to Sweet Valley."

"She got yours too?" Tom looked amused. "What do you want with those stupid things, Jessica?"

Jessica looked among the three guys. "You promise I can really have them? No backsies?"

"No backsies," Tom, Neil, and Todd said in unison.

"You guys are so stupid!" Jessica threw back her head and laughed. "Don't you know that the Home-o-Rama stores share a parent company with Gaudicci? I bet I can trade those gift certificates in for the perfect Italian leather back-to-school outfit!"

This has been my best summer ever, Jessica thought as everyone burst into laughter. And the fall was going to be even better. She was going back to school with one incredible new friend— and one incredible new outfit too!

Join Jessica and Elizabeth for the start of sophomore year and their big move to a cool off-campus duplex with hunky housemates Neil and Sam! It's time for new classes, new friends, new loves, new everything . . . starting with Sweet Valley University #51: LIVING TOGETHER.

Check out the **all-new....**

Sweet Valley Web site—

www.sweetvalley.com

New Features

Cool Prizes

The **ONLY** official Web site!

Hot Links

And much more!

BFYR 202

You'll always remember your first love.

Love Stories

Looking for signs he's ready to fall in love?

Want the guy's point of view?

Then you should check out *Love Stories*. Romantic stories that tell it like it is—why he doesn't call, how to ask him out, when to say good-bye.

Love Stories
Available wherever books are sold.